"Hey, Angela."

She didn't answer, but she did slow and stop to wait for whatever was coming next.

Jason continued. "If you're ever ready for me to call you, don't forget, you'll need to give me your number. And if you want to send me that picture of us, I'd love to have it."

She turned to stare over her shoulder. The desire to verbally hit him with something fun or flirty was on her face, along with a bit of extra pink, but she faced forward and walked away without satisfying either of them.

Still, the day had turned out to be a whole lot more fun than he'd expected.

The ache in his chest was familiar. It had been a long time since he'd hated watching a woman walk away, but that was where he was.

On his bench, like an old-timer, but fighting a junior high school type of crush.

Dear Reader,

My hero in *A Solder Saved* is a wounded vet named Jason Ward. He signs up for a college creative writing class to prove a point. I once did the same, but in my case it was because I loved to write. No one warned me that strangers would read and respond to my iffy poetry! Aloud! While I was still in the room! Of course, my hero aces his class. I did not, but I got some memories that make me laugh (even now) and I still love storytelling.

And writing mothers and daughters like Angela and Greer is a joy. My mother was a poet and my best friend no matter how many miles there were between us. She's on every page of this one. I hope you enjoy the story.

Cheryl

HEARTWARMING

A Soldier Saved

USA TODAY Bestselling Author

Cheryl Harper

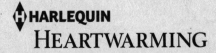

HARLEQUIN
HEARTWARMING

(H)HARLEQUIN®
HEARTWARMING™

ISBN-13: 978-1-335-88968-3

A Soldier Saved

Copyright © 2020 by Cheryl Harper

PLEASE RECYCLE
THIS PRODUCT IS RECYCLABLE

Recycling programs
for this product may
not exist in your area.

This edition published by arrangement with Harlequin Books S.A.

For questions and comments about the quality of this book, please contact us at CustomerService@Harlequin.com.

Harlequin Enterprises ULC
22 Adelaide St. West, 40th Floor
Toronto, Ontario M5H 4E3, Canada
www.Harlequin.com

Printed in U.S.A.

Cheryl Harper discovered her love for books and words as a little girl, thanks to a mother who made countless library trips, and an introduction to Laura Ingalls Wilder's Little House stories. Whether stories she reads are set in the prairie, the American West, Regency England or Earth a hundred years in the future, Cheryl enjoys strong characters who make her laugh. Now Cheryl spends her days searching for the right words while she stares out the window and her dog, Jack, snoozes beside her. And she considers herself very lucky to do so.

For more information about Cheryl's books, visit her online at cherylharperbooks.com or follow her on Twitter, @cherylharperbks.

Books by Cheryl Harper

Harlequin Heartwarming

Otter Lake Ranger Station

Her Unexpected Hero
Her Heart's Bargain
Saving the Single Dad
Smoky Mountain Sweethearts

Visit the Author Profile page
at Harlequin.com for more titles.

To old friends who are also family, thank you
for listening when I talk endlessly about
writing and understanding when I
Do Not Want To Talk About Writing.
Thank you for answering when I call.

CHAPTER ONE

"HEY, PROF, HEADS UP!" At the shouted warning, Dr. Angela Simmons hurried toward the steps in front of Sawgrass University's administration building. She brushed a bead of sweat off her forehead as she watched a group of rambunctious kids trot to their next target. The eternal game that raged in the center of campus, no matter how many students had already left for the summer, was similar to golf, but Frisbees hurled at a high rate of speed replaced dimpled golf balls.

Benches, lampposts, the hydrant near the corner of campus…those were the targets, and pedestrians were the hazards. At some point, the university would have to put in a dedicated course, but the lack of official equipment didn't slow down the game.

Freshman boys were enthusiastic about it. And loud.

Even at the end of May, when the heat should encourage more indoor games.

This sidewalk, the shadiest spot on campus, was always littered with kids in flip-flops, and the Monday before the first summer term started was no exception.

Since she'd fallen in deep, deep love with her job and the kids who came through her classes, Angela was happy there were plenty of students milling around the building that housed both the registrar and the campus bookstore.

Did she sometimes wish for a helmet for her own protection as she crossed from her parking spot to her office? Yes. But this building, the wide, tree-lined walkway leading up to it, and her beautiful office inside had convinced her Sawgrass University could be home.

"Play on, gentlemen," she called as she trotted up the low, flat steps leading to the building that was all angles and glass. Instead of brick and ivy and academic architecture, Sawgrass University's planners had gone all in on the mid-twentieth-century concepts of how the future would be built.

It had taken some adjustment, but Angela

had learned to appreciate the clean lines. The overwhelming white surfaces and the glint of sunshine blazing across the glass in the early afternoon could still stop her in her tracks.

Angela covered her eyes as she took the last steps and watched an older woman swing open the door and make the "hurry up" motion to the guy following slowly behind her. He did not walk faster.

"It's good advice to hurry," Angela said. "You never know when a stray Frisbee is aimed straight at whatever you're standing next to." She turned to encourage the man and stopped at his ferocious glare. It lasted only a second before all expression bleached from his face. Deep lines around his lips suggested pain or fatigue.

"Right. Sorry." He motioned to the older woman ahead of him and then waited patiently for Angela to follow her. Uncertain as to what she'd done to earn the hostile look, Angela hurried through the door and paused as the woman held out her hand.

"I was wondering…" Her voice was overly cheerful, but she turned a distinctly cold shoulder to the man stepping through the door behind them. When he braced an arm on the wall, Angela wondered if she should offer him a seat. "Could you give us directions to the registrar's office? My son needs to register for classes for the summer term. This stifling heat and that trek across campus have worn me out."

Angela would have bet all her money that the son was the one struggling. But she was happy to help. She pointed down the hallway and then noticed the scowl was back. Since he was pushing forty, she was certain she understood the source of some of the anger.

Her own daughter was sixteen and she'd insist her parents never follow her to school if she could get away with it. Since someone had to pay Greer's tuition, her ex still managed to tag along.

Even through the door that had closed behind them, Angela heard muffled shouts. The guys throwing the Frisbee had done something worth celebrating. It didn't take much.

"That's what I meant about hurrying. Disc golf gets pretty cutthroat around here. You don't want to be a casualty of a Frisbee to the head." Angela expected agreement or some kind of acknowledgment, but the woman gave her son a worried frown. He carefully straightened but did not speak.

"Directions?" his mother reminded them all, her eyebrows raised. "He needs to sign up before the office closes for the day." Did she regret asking for directions or the entire Sawgrass visit? Since her son had edged back toward the door and appeared ready to forget the whole thing, Mom needed to keep things moving.

Angela had been through snippy rants delivered by her own daughter, usually after embarrassing her at school, so she was sympathetic. The woman's son was struggling after the walk. He needed to sit down somewhere soon.

"Sure. You'll follow this hallway. About halfway down, another hall turns off to the right. Go all the way to the end. It's not too far. Someone there will help you get your classes set up." Angela shifted the strap of her briefcase on her shoulder. Should she offer to call someone to help them? "Welcome to Sawgrass. I hope you'll love it here."

The woman waved a hand. "Tell that to

him. He's convinced I'm torturing him. All I want him to do is take some accounting classes, do something safe for a while, you know?"

Safe? Her word choice stood out. Angela wasn't sure where all the tension between the two of them was coming from, but this guy? He was no accountant. His clothes were all right. Pressed khakis and a button-down were solid accounting wear, but his expression, the careful stare, even his too-long hair added up to *rugged* or even *rough*. Not *safe*. He agreed. The grimace was a big hint.

"Accounting is a good area. You passed the building all the business classes are in when you parked." Angela tipped her head to the side. "But part of the fun of the summer term is experimenting. Try something other than accounting. These are short, quick classes. If you're a freshman, it's awfully hard to know exactly what you want when you walk in the door."

She'd tried to tell Greer to keep her options open. It was impossible to know what would make her happy for the rest of her life at her age. This guy might have a better suggestion. Angela bent toward him. "Mothers don't know everything, even if we try to pretend we do."

He blinked slowly at her and then rubbed his forehead, as if the whole conversation was giving him a headache. "Thank you. Tell that to *her*." The words were polite. His tone was grim, but the corner of his mouth turned up.

Angela soaked in the air-conditioning as she watched them walk away. The woman was fluttering around her son while he made a slow, measured pace down the hall. Before Angela turned to climb the stairs to her office, he called, "If I decide to take your advice, what's the easiest class Sawgrass offers in the summer?"

Angela gripped the railing, one sneaker on the first step. "Hard to say. It depends on your interests and what you enjoy, but I've heard that an A is almost guaranteed in the Intro to Creative Writing class. And no matter what you do in the future, the ability to write well will serve you in the long run."

That was the sentence her own college advisor had delivered when Angela was a freshman. It had been good advice. The fact that she loved teaching creative writing above all else was a bonus.

If he chose her class, she might have one annoyed student on her hands.

He studied her for a second. "Writing?" He glanced at the papers rolled up into a tube in his right hand.

She dipped her head and then started up the stairs. The school administration took up the top floors of the building, but she'd garnered a plush office on the second floor.

When she reached the landing, her phone rang.

Pleased to have a moment to regain her breath after the climb, Angela dug her phone out of her briefcase.

"Hey, baby, give me a minute to unlock my office door. I'm almost there." Angela squeezed the cell phone between her ear and her shoulder. More people were on this floor, since the professors and teaching assistants, as well as admin people, were preparing for the summer semesters. It was a beautiful day to be almost anywhere else than inside, but it was hard to complain.

"Hello?" her daughter yelled through the

phone, so Angela quickly stepped into her office. "Are you still there, Mom?"

Sixteen was a trying age.

For everyone involved.

Angela dropped her bag on her desk and gripped the phone firmly. "Yes, Greer. Sorry, baby. It took me a minute longer to get to my office. A bunch of my colleagues are here, prepping for their classes and there was a bigger group for registration than I expected. So I had to dodge a few people in the hallway." And one handsome, grumpy guy. What was his story?

Opening the blinds was always Angela's first move. By virtue of her minor fame as a published poet and the university's desire to keep her happy, she had one of the prettiest views on campus. A small lake glimmered behind the ring of buildings that made up the main campus.

"Did you get my text?" Greer demanded. "You need to check out Dad's latest post. I mean now. Do it now."

"You were going to send a picture of your chemistry final grade. The test you were so nervous about? That's what I asked to see." Angela sat down and opened up her laptop. "I haven't had time to check your text yet. Why am I getting the feeling it's about something bigger than whether you made an A or a B? Whatever it is, we'll handle it." The emotion in her daughter's voice caught Angela's attention.

"Go to his page. You need to see the photos." Greer huffed out a breath. "I'm going to wait."

Angela navigated quickly to Rodney's page, determined to be upbeat and cheerful no matter what was waiting. The two of them hadn't been on easy speaking terms since he'd informed her of his last-minute long-weekend trip to Europe and his plan for their daughter to remain in Nashville. Alone.

Bringing Greer to Miami during the last weeks of school hadn't been an option. Greer had finals and parties and summer plans.

After the divorce, this was exactly what Angela had been afraid would happen, but she'd let Greer choose Nashville and her school and her friends over making the move to Miami with her. Accepting the offer at Sawgrass University had been difficult.

The only thing harder would have been staying at the same college where her ex-husband was the department chair.

"Okay, okay, okay, I'm there. On the page. Let me find your father's posts." Angela scrolled down quickly, certain she was going to find some extravagant purchase or a tale of woe that he'd split from Kate, the real estate lawyer he'd been dating for six months or so. He'd taken to being single again like the proverbial duck to water, dating soon after the divorce and often. Kate had lasted longer than most. Then the Eiffel Tower rolled past.

Paris. A weekend in Paris. That had been his plan.

And when she found the couple posed in front of the Eiffel Tower, the ring carefully displayed by their entangled fingers, her breath caught in her throat.

"They're engaged." Greer's quiet voice was the reminder Angela needed that she had to say something.

But what was there to say?

If she'd been pegged in the forehead by a flying Frisbee, she would be less stunned.

To buy herself a minute to catch up, Angela cleared her throat. "Well, that's great."

Her flat tone couldn't be fooling anyone, so she tried again. "An engagement and a once-in-a-lifetime trip. That's awesome. Are you mad they didn't include you?"

Angela wondered how bad the arrow to her heart would have hurt if Greer had been swept up into the extravagant event. At least she had company standing here on the outside. As it was, the bitter question about why Rodney had never taken her farther than Atlanta was better off ignored. He would have, if Angela had made all the plans, packed his suitcases and buckled his seat belt on the plane. The last part might be an exaggeration. "If they'd waited a month or so, you could have gone with them."

"A month? Not even. A week, Mom," Greer grumbled, a disappointed little girl seeping around the edges of weary maturity. "Did he choose the last weekend I couldn't go with them so I *couldn't go with them*?"

Angela slumped back in her chair. If they'd waited a week, she would have agreed to a European jaunt because Greer would have been so excited Angela would have had no other choice. The fact that Rodney had moved ahead without his daughter... There was something there, but Angela couldn't put her finger on it.

It was too spontaneous. Nothing like him.

"You can be disappointed and happy for them at the same time," Angela said as she scrolled.

"I am disappointed," Greer admitted, "but dragging a teenager along would seriously hamper the grand gesture, so I guess I'll let that go." Her daughter's heavy sigh cut across the distance, and Angela had no trouble picturing her familiar grimace of teenage angst. "But there's more you should know."

Angela inhaled slowly, her mind spinning as she evaluated possibilities and eliminated them. One wouldn't stay quiet.

It was the only answer that made sense of the hurried timing.

"She's pregnant." Angela rolled her pen across the desk as she absorbed that blow.

"Yeah," Greer said and then waited. "As soon as they got home, Dad told me. I haven't seen Kate since they left. I'm guessing that's because no one is sure how well I'm going to handle the news. They're moving her stuff in here this weekend."

Moving her stuff into the house Angela had shared with Rodney.

The same place Greer had and always would call home.

Angela braced her elbows on her desk and covered her eyes with one hand. In the short, world-changing conversation, her first worry had been for herself, but her daughter was going to be the one with the biggest challenge to face.

Switching from only child to big sister would take some adjustment.

Happy teen in a comfortable, spacious mansion to one sharing life with a new stepmother and a baby.

"It's a pretty big change," Angela said slowly. "How are you handling it?"

Greer groaned. "I'm confused." She didn't say anything else but the tense silence between them spoke for her daughter.

Angela wanted to jump in with solutions. That was who she was, who she had been for her whole relationship with Rodney Simmons.

That was why they were divorced. Happily divorced.

Still, Greer was her daughter, and solving

her problems was a part of a mother's job description. "Why don't you stay with me for the summer? You can have a break from normal. That might clear up some of the confusion." Angela straightened in her chair. If this development gave her a chance to spend more time with her daughter, it might have a silver lining. "We'll go to the beach. We'll make it to Key West finally. Just you and me, and when school's ready to start, you'll have had plenty of time to adjust."

"But the internship," Greer said. Angela was almost sure she could hear a flop, a loose thud of teenage girl bouncing on her mattress. "I worked so hard to get this job with Senator Gonzalez. Do you know how that will work in my favor when I'm applying to law school, Mom?"

Angela tightened her lips. In a world with some stereotypical lazy teens, Greer had been born with a keen sense of responsibility. And someone had taught her to plan for the future.

Rodney had been happy to follow all of Angela's plans until he'd faced forty and decided there was more to life than work.

More to life than the marriage they'd built and the family that Angela had sacrificed her own ambition to have. He'd risen to faculty chair, while she'd taken a ten-year break and then started at the bottom again.

But she did have Greer.

And the poetry. That break had meant the world to her poetry. That work had been what got her the job at Sawgrass, leading the English department. She'd never regret that time spent raising her daughter.

"Maybe there's something similar here," Angela said as she tried to come up with a match, but nothing sparked. Greer's father had met Senator Gonzalez at a university fund-raiser. Angela stayed near the refreshment table at fund-raisers because she wasn't a fan of schmoozing.

Refusing to examine how that might be another good reason her ex had risen faster in his career than she had, Angela bit her lip and reconsidered her suggestion to Greer. "Or not. If you came here, you'd spend the summer stuck in my house or working retail while I teach summer term and deal with preparations for the fall. Staying in Nashville is the smart thing to do. But we don't always have to be so smart, G." They didn't. That was what she'd learned about the same time her husband had changed his mind about their marriage. It was only a working theory, however. She hadn't done much to test it.

"Really? We don't have to be smart?" Her daughter's drawl eased some of Angela's worry. "That's kind of our thing, the whole family. Who are you and what have you done with Dr. Angela Simmons, shining star at Sawgrass University?"

Angela shook her head. "Sometimes I wish I could unteach you some of the things we worked so hard to give you. Life is short. You need to enjoy it." When she turned eighteen, Greer shouldn't have to pick the career that would last her whole life. She should know how to have fun while she was still young.

"I want to come to Miami. I do," Greer said, "but how hurt would Dad be if I did that? And Kate? She's nice, even if I'm not quite ready to welcome a new brother or sister. I've been to Senator Gonzalez's office already and it's what I always imagined, so…"

Angela rolled the pen across her desk again. She wanted to fight, but the one promise she'd made to herself after the divorce was that Greer would make her own decisions. She'd chosen to stay in Nashville to complete high school. She'd chosen not to leave her friends or her father, and it was working out well. She and Greer spent weeks together during breaks and talked on the phone at least once every day. Once Greer graduated, Angela would press harder to become her home base.

Or that had been the plan.

With a baby brother or sister on the way, that plan was in danger.

"I didn't mean to derail your whole day. What are you doing at work today?" Greer asked. "Any handsome freshmen boys I need to know about?"

Angela laughed as the image of the guy she'd nearly pulled inside the doors downstairs popped into her brain. Handsome? Oh yeah. Boy? Definitely not. "Nah. I'll keep my eyes open for you, though."

"I'm hoping that means they're all on the East Coast in some Ivy League towns." Greer had planned for as long as Angela could remember to get into the best university. Which one that was changed now and then, but they all had East Coast addresses.

"Which one are we targeting this month?" Angela asked, grateful for a change in subject.

"Senator Gonzalez is a Princeton graduate. I figure he can give me the inside scoop to help me move it up the list or cross it off completely." Angela and Rodney had both done fine at state schools, but obviously Senator Gonzalez was going to be the expert on hand.

The knock on the door on Greer's end of the phone was loud and clear. "Just a minute, Dad." She waited a second before returning to the call. "Dad's going to drop me at Senator Gonzalez's office to fill out some paperwork, so I gotta go. Wish I knew what I was going to say to Dad."

Angela closed her eyes. She wanted to help Greer, but she was also so relieved not to be in the same spot. Eventually, she'd have to congratulate her ex, but not yet. "Be honest with him but remember that he loves you, G. This is all going to work out. You will love being a big sister." Angela hoped it was true. Greer was smart and responsible and yet so young. The road might be bumpy.

"Are you going to be okay, Mom?" Greer asked, her voice tentative, as if she wanted to know the answer but was scared to ask the question.

"Yes, ma'am, I'll be fine. It's a beautiful day here in Florida, hot enough to make you sweat inside a full-size freezer, with beautiful sunshine and enough students wandering around to keep me busy for a few weeks." Angela made sure she said every word through a smile because the last thing she wanted was her daughter worrying about her. "You take your time with all these changes. It's going to work out. You'll see."

Greer didn't answer at first. Eventually, as Angela was gearing up to contribute something else, her daughter said, "It would be cool if you had an awesome date for the wedding."

It might be cool, but it wasn't going to happen. Until that second, Angela hadn't even considered attending the wedding. She rested her head against the desk. Before the summer was over, would she be wishing Rodney and Kate all the best in person? Great.

Why hadn't she started dating before the ink on the divorce decree was dry? Rodney had.

Oh yeah. The job. The career. The move. Enjoying the freedom to make plans for one for the first time in a long time.

Greer was young and as romantic as most teenage girls. She'd never understand that.

"Um, well, I guess, but…" Angela wasn't sure about the rest of that statement, so she let it sit there, a big old nothing in the middle of all the unsaid words that paused outside of the frame.

"They haven't announced the date yet, but it'll be before school starts again." Greer hesitated before she added the last part. "Early August was mentioned."

Two months. The idea that it would be that soon had never occurred to Angela. Why? Because she didn't want to study any of this too closely.

"Before school starts again." It made sense. If this weird Parisian jaunt had been out of character for her ex-husband, wanting to be married before the baby came fit his new character perfectly. "Okay. I'll keep my eyes open for a suitable guy. How's that?"

Muttering the words knocked her pulse up a notch.

Actually carrying through with that? Not going to happen. If she went, she'd go solo. There was nothing wrong with that.

Did ex-wives attend weddings of ex-husbands?

It depended on the split.

And the sinking sensation in the pit of Angela's stomach convinced her that an invitation to the wedding would arrive.

She'd have to attend. If the school term was eliminated as a reasonable answer, she had no plausible excuse.

"Check out the other professors. There's got to be a cute one somewhere on campus. He'd be an idiot not to accept your dinner invitation, but you should get a move on. Inviting dates to weddings is one of those things you only do with someone you've been dating for a while. Otherwise, they assume you're hoping for a ring yourself. You only have a couple of months."

"How do you know this? You might as well be a dating expert, and I am certain your parents only allowed you to start dating this spring." Angela closed her eyes and tried to stifle the words that might have an edge of irritation to them.

"Mom." That was Greer's only answer. She wasn't entertaining any of this foolishness.

"I'll keep my eyes open, okay, boss?" Angela offered. "But how many times have I told you to be the hero of your own story. No sidekick required."

Her daughter's groan eased some of Angela's worry. "I'm watching out for you, but you're not going to listen to me, are you?" The last word was a dramatic, drawn-out wail that was sixteen all the way to its core.

"If I go alone, they'll sit me at the kids' table. I'll be happy there." It would be there or with the collection of odds and ends gathered together at one table in a dark corner.

And no matter what, it would be okay. She'd get to visit Greer. That would make it all worthwhile.

"They mentioned a destination wedding— I hope it's in Paris," Greer said.

"Go do your paperwork. Get your internship. Remember that your father loves you and that you're going to be an awesome big sister. Whatever destination it is will be fun.

We will make sure of that. This is all going to work out. I promise." Saying it strengthened her own confidence.

Greer's "Okay" had a distinct tone of "If you say so" that implied she wasn't sure.

"I say so. Call me later and tell me all about the senator's office." Angela ended the call after Greer's usual "loveyoubye" and put her phone next to her computer.

Before she could stop, one finger slowly scrolled through her ex-husband's page. The photos in Paris were beautiful. Every picture of him and his bride-to-be shouted romance and happily-ever-after.

Angela bent forward to study the photo. No baby bump. Not yet.

When she realized how invested she was getting and how each new photo hammered harder on the "I don't measure up" spike, she closed the lid of her laptop and turned to stare out the window at the lake.

She lost track of time as the possibilities floated through her head. She might not even be invited to this destination wedding. What a relief that would be. If she didn't have to put on a brave, independent face, all of this would be easier.

But she wanted time with Greer.

"It's time to plan a trip to Nashville." Angela tangled her fingers over her stomach and frowned at the lake. She hated going back. Her whole world had been turned on its head, but the city where she'd spent the biggest part of her adult life went on without her. Greer kept growing. Life kept going.

And in Miami, nothing changed. Ever. She worked the job she loved. Teaching the classes she wanted to teach was fulfilling. Her condo with a view of the beach was small but it was comfortable. If her life was a body of water, it was the lake outside her window. Nothing much disturbed the surface.

Except her ex-husband had chucked a big rock right in the middle and the ripples were going to spread.

"Great metaphor, prof," Angela muttered to herself. "You should be a creative writing teacher." She spun her desk chair back around and reopened her laptop. She quickly closed the window on Rodney's page because there was nothing she could do about that.

Her lake was here and now and she needed a completed syllabus before class started. Everything else could wait because she had work to do.

CHAPTER TWO

JASON WARD HAD helped gather intelligence on several dangerous strongholds in his career. Elementary schools that had been commandeered by rebels. Money-laundering facilities built and staffed by terrorists. The crowded base commissary on payday.

Neither the all-white, chrome-and-glass buildings of Sawgrass University nor the red-tiled roofs of the Concord Court townhome complex should have provoked the adrenaline spikes that were unraveling his last nerve.

Adrenaline had gotten him this far. The walk across campus had been a test of his steadiness and stamina, but he'd made it. Unfortunately, that surge of energy was gone. Now he wanted to sit somewhere still and cool forever.

"Spanish mission style. That's what they call this."

Jason did not glance at the driver's seat. They'd managed to stick to neutral topics during the quick ride from the university to this parking spot in front of the leasing office of Concord Court, but his mother was half a second from disaster.

He couldn't lose his temper. He owed her too much.

It was a good thing the traffic had been light, for more than one reason.

His mother drove his truck like it was as big as a semi, perched close and clenching the steering wheel with both hands.

And their blowup had been building. Too much time to discuss anything other than the weather was dangerous. In southern Florida, talking about the weather didn't take long. It didn't vary much. Hot. Humid. Storm in the afternoon.

Like the one that was gathering slowly in dark clouds rolling off the ocean. He needed to get this all finished before the storm hit. Tripping was too common right now even without wet sidewalks to give him trouble.

"Spanish mission. Good to know." Jason gripped the door handle tightly and then forced his hands into his lap. "I'll be sure to drop that fact in conversation wherever I can work it in."

Out of the corner of his eye, he could see the tight knot her arms made across her chest grow smaller, but she didn't snap. Not yet.

That was driving him up the wall. They were both on their best behavior. It couldn't last. They'd made it through his recovery in the hospital, and the time he'd spent in her new spare bedroom while he was suffering rehab. They were about to have some breathing room, each with their own space again.

All he had to do was pick up his keys.

They did so much better with half the world between them and nothing but phone lines open.

"You know I'm a big boy, Mama. What about all the fun, retiree things you could be doing in your new assisted-living facility instead of escorting me up to meet the teacher on my first day of school. I didn't even need a lunchbox or a backpack today." Jason winced. If the men he'd led saw him now, huddled in the passenger seat of his pride-and-joy pickup, with his mommy to hold his hand and in full possession of the steering wheel, how much grief would they give him? So much.

All of it done in love, of course, but the nicknames this would earn him would be embarrassing.

There'd be no more trash talk from them, though. All he'd had to do was lose part of his leg. He'd gotten a one-way ticket home while his crew went on without him.

"Do you remember the last time I accepted your word that you were going to go out and do something that could possibly change your entire life?" his mother drawled and held up her hand before he could answer. "Because I do. I remember it sometimes as a bad dream that wakes me up because I can't breathe in my own bed at night. I sent you out to enroll in community college. We discussed a degree in business management. What did you do instead?"

She didn't need him to answer. It was a waste of time to try because they'd had this conversation more than once since he'd woken up stateside.

Mae Ward was stubborn. She'd wait for him to try to answer, so he opened his mouth and she immediately said, "Instead of community college, you enlisted. A foolish, brave boy, you did it without talking to me or to your father because…" She tapped her finger to her lip. "Why was it again?"

Jason cleared his throat. "Because I knew what I wanted for my life." He'd done it without discussing it with them because he'd known there was no way to convince them to agree.

"To get out of Nowhere, Georgia." Her head jerked as if she was agreeing that she recalled the same conversation in the same manner. "And not in two years or four, but to get out of Rosette, the only home you ever had, immediately. Look how well that turned out. You could have died. More than once. Forgive me if I don't fall for that again." She slowly turned her head and narrowed her eyes at him. "Fool me once, I'll never forget it and make you regret it at the first opportunity. That's how the saying goes, isn't it?"

"Can't happen again. Absolutely no one is recruiting middle-aged amputees."

"Employers are always recruiting people with the right skills," his mother said brightly.

At least she was talking again. This was

the mother he remembered. She'd been spookily kind since he'd been hospitalized stateside.

"It was a car accident. Not a bullet, not a bomb. A split-second mistake that overturned the tactical truck I was in. Crashes happen here, too, Mama." The accident responsible for crushing his lower left leg had occurred during an ambush, and whether he'd make it out alive had been touch and go. Jason closed his eyes and tried to count to ten. His mother didn't need to hear that and he didn't want to talk about it anymore. Ever. "I've already enrolled at Sawgrass University. You were there. Don't you remember the kid giving me the 'you gotta be kidding me' stare when you asked about what sort of meals the cafeteria served?"

Her shrug was small to match how little she cared about his big-boy emotions. "You need to regain your strength, JJ. You can't do that on terrible food. That hospital? I could not believe how many times they brought you asparagus." She snorted. "Asparagus! For a wounded man. A national hero!"

Her outrage was amusing, but there was a whole lot of anger underneath it.

Too much of it belonged squarely on his shoulders. "National hero" was enough to make his stomach cramp, too. It wasn't true. He wished it was, but he'd been in the wrong place at the wrong time.

His mother had been ready to go to war over the food in the hospital. Neither one of them was going to bring up the showdown she'd had with the unlucky woman who'd delivered lunch the second week he'd been there. He'd managed to talk his mother out of objecting on the first asparagus day. On the second, she'd settled for muttering under her breath and a trip to the vending machine to get him chips. That third day? Vegetables had gone into the trash can, and his mother's voice had climbed to the roof.

No more asparagus was delivered, and he'd noticed an uptick in everyone's efforts to get him released from the hospital.

He owed her a lot.

"Thank you, Mama. For everything." He watched her eyebrows rise. He should express gratitude more often. "You never left me when I needed you, but this? I've got this under control. I hate that you rented the house out. You aren't ready for an assisted-living facility, are you?" He hadn't recovered from the shock of listening to her give a new mailing address and phone number at the hospital. It was local. After two decades of distance, he and his mother were going to be living in the same town.

Luckily, Miami was big enough for the both of them. Probably.

"I did that for you—of course I did." Mae Ward shook her finger. "And what if I didn't want to spend the rest of my life in a wide spot in the road, either? I've done quite enough of cleaning those same wood floors and weeding that blasted flower garden your daddy loved. Somebody else can do it." She shrugged. "Or they won't, but they won't experience an ounce of guilt over it, either. Not like I have. Rosette will go on. You and me, we're setting down new roots."

"Well…" Caught off guard at the suggestion that his mother, a woman born, raised, married and widowed in the same small town, might not have been perfectly content with the situation, Jason studied the red-tiled roof and warm tan stucco of the complex's office building.

"That is a deep subject, young man." His

mother patted his shoulder and waited for him to acknowledge her small, worn-out joke. "We both need new horizons. I've always dreamed of living on the water, so I could not be happier with my little apartment with a view of Snapper Creek. In two weeks or so, you'll be up to driving yourself, I'll be learning to play golf and drive a golf cart, and this whole thing is going to turn out to be a grand adventure. Stop worrying so much."

Jason blinked slowly as he let that soak through him. His mother was telling him not to worry.

Even if the shoe being on the other foot pinched, she was absolutely right.

So what if he didn't know what he wanted to do for the rest of his life or even after he managed to get his mother out of his hair that afternoon? Well, it was frustrating.

After decades of service to the United States government, he was absolutely free of constraints. He'd expected to be happy with all the freedom someday, when he was ready to retire. Now? He was glad he had a college class to look forward to, even if it was creative writing and he'd only signed up to keep the peace.

At least Concord Court was no run-down old folks' home where the government might stash worn-out soldiers. He'd been afraid of that. This place was well looked after and comfortable. He could get on his feet here.

"Let's get out of this truck. I was so tense driving this thing I got a permanent crick in my neck." His mother yanked the keys out of the ignition and handed them over. "Next thing on my list is to lease me a cute little convertible. Let the wind blow through my hair." She tapped the straw hat she'd been wearing ever since she crossed the Florida state line as far as he knew. "It's time we both shook things up. I got things I want to do, and the clock is ticking."

Before he could ask for more information, his mother shoved open the door and dropped to stand on the pavement. The heat invaded the cab of the truck immediately, and he lost any interest in continuing the conversation until there was air-conditioning involved.

"Need help?" she asked before she slammed her door shut. The worry in her eyes was almost completely hidden away. He wondered how much it was costing her to keep it all contained.

He didn't want help, and he was going to pretend he didn't need it.

"Nope. Got it." He opened his own door and did the easy part first. His right leg, the one that would now forever be known as the good one, moved almost as it had his whole life. But the left leg was useless.

"Don't you lift that with your hand. That pretty little girl in physical therapy told you more than once it should be doing work all on its own at this point." His mother had crossed behind the truck to watch him, her arms held out as if she had any hope of catching him if he started to fall. They'd already tried that two or three times, and he'd landed in a heap on the ground.

"I wasn't." He'd been about to do that very thing, but taking shortcuts was never worth the trouble.

Focus. The weakness in his left leg made him so angry. That rage should release enough adrenaline to get him out of the truck. It rolled under his skin, raising his temperature, making it hard to breathe normally. With fits and starts, he managed to swing his left leg around. The pain was lessening every day, but the weakness…

Embarrassed and frustrated and mad at himself and the world, Jason had to force himself to take deep breaths when he was standing outside the truck. One split-second accident and his whole life was over.

"You did it." His mother's expressionless face was all that saved him from cursing or kicking. "And the next time, it'll be easier. You'll see." Then she stepped up on the sidewalk and motioned him to hurry. "It's too hot to be standing around outside."

"Well, go inside, then. I need a minute," Jason snapped before he could stop.

"Throwing yourself a pity party, I expect." Her grumbling as she marched away surprised a smile from him.

Jason stepped carefully to be sure the prosthesis would hold him—the searing numbness in his knee was familiar and enough to remind him that life went on.

His life hadn't ended, and a bigger, better person wouldn't let self-pity stop him in his tracks. Fingers crossed that someday he might be that person.

"Get on with it, Ward." He said the words, but the tone was his father all the way. None of this pity nonsense. Life was meant for living.

He carefully stepped up on the sidewalk, and some of the tension in his shoulders subsided. His mother was focused on the lush foliage making up a privacy screen around a sparkling pool, which was nestled in the large courtyard formed by the five buildings of the complex. A wrought iron fence with intricate gates surrounded it.

Nice.

Concord Court had been built to be more than a sterile rehabilitation facility. This was meant to be a home, one a man could be proud to claim.

"For a woman who was complaining about the size of a garden, you sure are interested in that—" Jason had no idea what it was called "—bushy, flowery thing."

His mother shook his head. "Bougainvillea."

"Hmm." Jason stopped beside her. "'Bushy, flowery thing' is easier to say." He pointed at a large bright orange bud. "And that one?"

"Hibiscus." His mother gestured broadly. "I appreciate a smart garden that someone else weeds. It's called civilization. Welcome to civilization."

She was right about that.

Jason studied the shaded walkways that led off from the pool to the different clusters of townhomes. The whole place was quiet. He suspected there weren't too many kids or families here.

Still, it was nice. Peaceful. For two years, he'd stay here and have plenty of time to figure out what he wanted for the rest of his life, such as it was. Maybe his mother was right and college would help.

"You're Jason Ward, right?" a woman said from the doorway to the office. "Your appointment was for ten minutes ago."

The firm, no-nonsense delivery had him snapping to attention. That quick response had served him well in the military. He hadn't expected to need it this afternoon at Concord Court.

The frown on the woman's face suggested she was used to compliance.

"Yes. Sorry we're late. I had…" Second thoughts? An attack of the poor-me in the parking lot?

It didn't matter how he intended to complete the sentence, because she was too busy to wait. "I'm Reyna Montero, the manager of Concord Court, and I have another appointment in half an hour, so let's get the paperwork completed." She didn't wait for his answer or for him to enter the office. The door swung slowly closed and they watched through a large window as she moved behind a desk.

"Good thing you're used to military manners," his mother said as her lips twitched.

Jason met her eyes as he held the door open, worried how his mother might react to someone being abrupt with her wounded chick, but she settled on a stool at the small counter and picked up a magazine.

That way she could eavesdrop, never miss a thing and still say he was overreacting when he complained about whatever trouble she might stir up.

"Start with these. Name, phone number, emergency contact." Reyna slid a sheaf of forms across to him. "Standard stuff. Rules of the complex here, hours of operation." She didn't wait for him to comply with orders but moved on to the smaller stack of paper in her hands. "We have some of your records on file. Please review them. You were referred by the surgeon at the veterans' hospital. You've got physical therapy to finish, and then what?"

Jason was working on printing neatly because he knew a mess would not be tolerated, so it took a second to realize she was waiting for him to answer.

"What?" he asked, certain he was about to get a dressing-down.

"After you finish physical therapy, what are your plans?" Reyna leaned back in her chair. "As you know, part of the agreement is that you are making plans. You're passing through here. Veterans from all branches of service are welcome after they leave active duty, but only temporarily. Find a job. Improve your work skills. Get a degree. Recover and move on. That's your mission now. Two years and you're out. That's plenty of time to get your feet under you."

Would making a joke that it was only one foot now make things better or worse?

Fatigue settled in again. He didn't have any energy for joking.

"I've already registered at Sawgrass University. I'm taking a class this summer, and

I'll decide whether to enroll in more classes for the fall semester." He waited for his mother to chime in that he'd be enrolling if she had anything to say about it, but she was blessedly silent.

Reyna nodded. "Perfect. That's all we ask. Go to school. Go to work. Whatever makes you happy. We're here to help you find that thing, what you are meant to do after the military. In your welcome packet, you'll find information about our services. Lots of help available, tutors, support groups, all of it listed there. I have an email list. I'll update you as we add services. Next up is a job counselor who can help with applications and résumés. Any other assistance you need, let me know." She returned to her paperwork, her manner completely at odds with the promise of her words.

Jason watched her for a minute. He'd met a few like her, women who'd battled alongside him in the worst circumstances.

"Which branch?" he asked.

She glanced up. "Air force." One corner of her mouth turned up. "The best one." She opened a drawer and slid two keys across the desk to him. "If you want to drive around, you'll be on the east side." She pointed through the window. "I'll meet you there to do the walk-through of your unit. I hope you'll find whatever you need here, Ward."

Jason picked up the keys, stunned at how easy it had been. "You don't need a deposit or…" There had to be something else.

"Not for two years. Leave the place better than you found it." She tilted her chin up. "You're going to find men and women in all kinds of situations here, Ward. A guy like you, one who's healthy and mostly in one piece, you can help others. That's why I'm here."

Mostly one piece. It was an interesting way to say, "Get on with it," but he appreciated the sentiment.

"Right now, I've got my hands full taking care of me." He held the door open for Reyna, who narrowed her eyes at his answer. Ignoring his mother's shaking head, he stepped outside. He'd never turned down a request for help, not that Reyna had made it optional. His whole life, he'd been the first in line for the hard job.

But he wasn't the same man he'd been.

As they walked to the car, he noticed that

Reyna hadn't waited for them and she wasn't hesitating a second. He and his mother had better get a move on or Reyna might decide he wasn't motivated enough and change the locks before they made it to the townhouse.

His mother took the keys and started the truck. In his hurry, sliding back into the truck had been easy. Seamless. As if he'd been doing it his whole life.

Concord Court had been even easier. Enrolling at Sawgrass had gone without a hitch, too.

For that matter, his first conversation with a pretty woman that day, the one who'd suggested the creative writing class that he'd enrolled in to irritate his mother, had gone well. There was hope that not every female at Sawgrass would make him feel ancient. Her smile had almost been enough to cut through his black cloud.

He'd had some bad luck, but it was going to turn.

Getting it to stick around long enough for him to come to terms with his new body would be the challenge.

CHAPTER THREE

FIVE MINUTES BEFORE her Introduction to Creative Writing class started, Angela stood up from her desk, the tumble of excited butterflies a familiar side effect of the beginning of a new semester. She loved teaching, and this was her favorite class of all time. The condensed timeline of the summer session meant she had to hit the ground running, another challenge that she loved.

"Be firm. Fair." She clenched and unclenched her hands a few times to ground herself in the moment. Trotting in, prepared to do somersaults in joy, would weaken her authority. It would also confuse her students, who were likely not nearly as excited to be in the classroom.

Angela inhaled slowly and then took twice as long to exhale before picking up the copies of the syllabus she'd made and the thumb drive with all of her class presentations. No book needed. Materials could change according to her whim and developments in modern creative writing.

"Better get to it or you'll be late, prof," Angela muttered to herself as she rounded the desk. As she walked down the hall, the echo of her heels clattering on the empty hallway, she settled. Other things might be frayed, those threads around the edges of her life. She still hadn't come to terms with her ex-husband's good news, even after almost a week of being drawn to check all his social media posts like a thief returning to the scene of the crime. Greer was slowly coming around, but her satisfaction with her internship and her new hero's attention had cast a rosy glow over everything for days. For some reason, listening to "Senator Gonzalez says" over and over had contributed to Angela's dissatisfaction with her own situation, but she was adjusting to that, too. Slowly.

Her daughter was doing fine without her. That had always been the goal of parenting, even if it had arrived sooner than she'd anticipated.

None of that mattered right this minute.

She was a great teacher. This was what she was meant to do.

When she made it to the classroom on the first floor, Angela braced a straight arm against the door and shoved it open. "Good morning, class. I'm Dr. Angela Simmons, and this is Introduction to Creative Writing. If you're supposed to be in a biology or chemistry class, boy, have you come to the wrong place."

She stopped behind the podium at the front of the room and set her stack down with a plop. She was expecting twelve students, so she did a head count, her eyes moving rapidly until she landed on the angry guy from registration. Off and on, whenever his image would pop into her mind as she worked, Angela had calculated the odds that he would take her advice.

And here he was.

As a professor, she was happy.

As a mother, it was discouraging to understand that Greer might never grow to the age where she stopped doing things only to show her mother she could. This guy? He had to be near forty, and he'd registered for her class because it wasn't accounting.

And as a woman, Angela had to admit that the spark of excitement she was experiencing was more than the normal first day of class warranted.

Because she had spent more time than she was comfortable with wondering if he'd show up. Now that he had, she'd have to figure out why she was thinking about him and what to do about it.

As their eyes met, he raised his eyebrows. That was his only reaction.

Given the state of his stiff posture, the crisp edges of his starched button-down and the polish on his loafers, Angela would guess he kept things pretty tightly controlled. Even his jeans had crisp creases that suggested they'd been ironed.

In a room filled with lounging kids in flip-flops and T-shirts, he was the odd man out. Only his hair—dark blond and longer than she'd expect from such a precise guy, and messy as if he'd already run his fingers through it in frustration—matched the general laid-back style of college students.

"First thing we do is move all these desks. I need a semicircle with my chair and podium at the center." Angela pulled her chair away from the wall and then motioned at her audience, who had not moved an inch. "Now. Move your desks into a circle." She waved her arms broadly, and the loud clatter of the scramble to follow her directions filled the air.

When all the dust settled again, she was directly opposite Mr. Starch, who might hate every minute of her *creative* writing class. At this vantage point, she'd have a good view of his face, which was hard to read. Instead of the pain and fatigue she'd seen on his face at registration, all she could see was calm.

Since the whole class was now waiting on her to do something, she had to get her head back in the game.

"Take a syllabus and pass the stack to your neighbor." Angela reached up to put the thumb drive in the laptop that ran the A/V in the room and picked up the remote. "First question and every answer gets a point." Students were crazy for points. After all, lots of points meant better grades. Still, they came in the door anxious to find the quickest way to beat the grading system. "Why are you here?"

This process always went the same way. The two or three overachievers who were either trying to pad their grades or graduate early raised their hands and immediately gave polished, inoffensive answers. To broaden their writing skill. To gain useful knowledge.

There were always a few whose inspiration wasn't clear—she wondered how they made the decision to get out of bed in the morning. Those students usually shrugged. They had to enroll in something.

It was easy to forgive both of those groups, since there were always one or two people who had the spark, the wonder or fear or hope that this could be what they were searching for, the thing that convinced them it was okay to need to write. Those kids she'd love until the day she withered into dust like the frail pages of an original folio of Shakespeare's sonnets.

She waited until the flurry of answers died down.

That left Mr. Starch. The wild card. He cared too much about his appearance to be in the don't-care group, but the true overachiever would never have asked the question he had at registration. True over-achievers might want the easy A, but they wouldn't advertise the fact.

She pointed at him. "First name, please."

"Jason," he answered in a rough rumble. Calling on him was a gamble. That might be enough to send him running for the hills. "And I'm here because someone suggested I try it."

Someone. She met his stare, and he dipped his chin as if to acknowledge her look. He wasn't going to back down. It appeared he also refused to call her out. This would be fun.

"Five weeks. That's all we have here. Five weeks for you to learn about the forms that creative writing takes, to give it a shot, experiment, find out what works for you and what doesn't, and most important, to experience the terror of having someone else read what you wrote. Out loud. In public. Where everyone can love it or hate it."

She crossed her legs and was more gratified than she should have been that Mr. Starch noticed. His eyes drifted down before snapping back to her face. The two of them had dressed for success instead of comfort.

Dressing in her professorial best, a suit and heels, on the first day was about setting expectations. Today, it had the bonus of making her look and feel like a boss.

"Terror," drawled the surfer dude who she would guess had aspirations of being a business mogul and was planning to hang out in a writing course. "Terror? That can't be right. This is the easiest A on campus." As he slumped forward in his seat, his expression suggested he was annoyed at the miscommunication.

"I was wondering when this might come up, so thank you for being honest." Angela pulled up her roster of students. "Your name is?"

He straightened his shoulders and tugged on the edge of his Sawgrass T-shirt. "Brad." No last name. As if that would protect him.

"Right. Brad Oliver." Angela made a check mark, not that it meant anything or mattered. "If I worried about points, I'd give you another point for that, Brad. Good job." He didn't appear to be reassured. When she explained the difference of her grading system for this class, students always grew *more* anxious. "No points in this class.

Here's how you get an easy A." She cleared her throat and absorbed the silence in the room. Why was this so much fun? Hard to say, but if she had to guess, there was only one other person in the room who understood how much she was enjoying herself. Mr. Starch had relaxed a bit in his seat, as if he was liking the show.

Jason. That was his name. She checked her list. Jason Ward.

"It really is as easy as this." Angela advanced her PowerPoint to the slide titled "So You Want to Make an A." It was the only slide about grades. "Do the work. Over five weeks, we will cover some basic and broad distinctions in creative writing. Poetry. Flash fiction. Creative nonfiction. We will glance briefly at movie reviews and travel writing. I've given you a list of reading. It's all available with an easy web search.

"You will turn in four pieces of your own writing. The first will be a poem. The last will be the summary and first chapter of a novel of whatever genre you choose. They will be anonymous when they are distributed, but as a class, we will read them. The other assignments are your choice. We will critique them. You will make the decision whether to own your writing and defend it or talk about what your intentions were after we read it. That's where the terror comes in."

She always paused here for emphasis.

"Yes, it's possible to be no good at this. It really is." Angela made sure she met each person's eyes. "It's not easy listening to other people judge the words you put on paper. It never is, and the more you care, the harder it gets." She shrugged. "But if you want to write, you've got to come to terms with it. Every piece you write will be an improvement. And those of you who said it would be a good skill for whatever you do, you were right. This is a skill you'll need in the corporate world or running your own business. Putting yourself out there and learning to roll with whatever the world gives you back? Man, that's the lesson of a lifetime."

Angela hoped her words were sinking in. Her eyes met Jason's across the circle.

In two short encounters, she'd seen him irritated and amused. His face was absolutely sober now. The two of them were old enough to understand that sometimes rolling with the punches wasn't that easy. Sometimes the world knocked a person down.

"Do the work. Come to class. Join the discussion. Get your A." Angela sighed. "Along the way, you'll learn something. Easy."

If the full dozen made it to the end of the semester, it would be unusual. In the fall and spring semesters, the attrition rate was low. In these summer semesters, there was little time to gear up for the public criticism, and she'd lose several to the pressure before the semester was over. The ones who stayed would be better for it.

"First up. Everybody loves poetry, right?" Angela grinned at the mix of disgruntled faces staring back at her. They only thought they hated poetry. She could teach them differently. "Some of it rhymes, a lot of it doesn't, but what you can count on is imagery and the rhythm of language and the choices you make. It's often condensed, so each word demands power. Somebody name your favorite poet."

Silence was heavy at this point. The first student she'd noticed with a spark raised her hand and Angela motioned her to lower it.

"Spit it out. Don't interrupt each other, but I'm asking for your input here."

The student tugged uncertainly on a braid hanging over her shoulder. "I enjoy reading black poets. Maya Angelou or Nikki Giovanni."

Angela clasped her hands together, thrilled to have at least one reader. "Good answers, good examples of how word choice and the cadence of language affects tone in poetry. What's your name?"

"Nikki." She wrinkled her nose. "My mom is a fan, too."

"Awesome, Nikki." After checking her class roster, Angela nodded. "My mom used to read poetry to me. That's how I learned to love it. Her favorite? Edna St. Vincent Millay. Edna. Angela. They aren't so far apart, I guess, but I'm glad she didn't name me after Edna. My favorite poet changes by the day. Nikki is a great name. Nikki Giovanni writes with power and intensity. Maybe you will, too." The girl's smile bloomed broader as she pushed her braids over her shoulder. She was one to watch. Nikki already had the spark. All she needed was oxygen to feed the fire. "Who else has a favorite?"

She heard the usuals. Emily Dickinson. Langston Hughes. Shakespeare. All worthy choices that had been thoroughly covered in high school English classes.

Finally, Jason straightened, and Angela felt the tingle all the way down her spine. This was going to be good.

"Do song lyrics count?" he asked, that rough edge of his voice sharpening her attention and her interest.

Student. He's a student.

Angela wanted to pat him on the shoulder or encourage this. Clapping would be unacceptable. For some reason, maybe it was the roughness of his voice or his starchy outside, but she had the impression Jason didn't open himself up to being wrong often, and he'd done it.

"Of course, song lyrics count," Angela said. "One of the most amazing pieces of creative writing and poetry to me? Rap. Old-school, new, whatever. The way words flow and build a beat in your head and commit images to memory. That's poetry. Country, bluegrass, folk music from the sixties… There's a story being told in images. Before we wrote things down, we memorized stories with beats and mental pictures and words."

She hoped Jason would be one of the students to make it all the way to the end of the semester. Whatever he was controlling, the piece of him that was asking for guidance in the hallway of a college administration building, it was going to be interesting to get to know.

"So, Jason, what music speaks to you?" Angela asked, prepared to agree with whatever came out of his mouth. Even death metal would have some kind of connection if she dug deep.

"Lots of music, but based on your description of images and the power of the words..." He paused.

Was he regretting his decision to step out? She hoped not. This was all part of the process.

"Smokey." He cleared his throat. "Smokey Robinson. 'My Girl.' It gets at the way love, especially when it's new, makes a man float, bright and warm, sunshiny. He's bouncing along and ready to tell the world." His lips tightened. "Maybe."

In the seconds before she could answer,

Angela realized she'd tangled her fingers together in a hard knot.

As if the anticipation had been too much. But his answer… She hadn't expected it.

"Smokey. What a great answer." She stood to pace while she tried to get a handle on the fizz of excitement that percolated inside. "And that's it exactly. The words. The music. Everything works together to create emotion. The poet or songwriter makes careful choices to give you that bubble and the connection that crosses time and location because it's part of being human. With Smokey, you also have the joy of his voice, which brings to mind the difference between reading a poet's words and hearing them spoken. Poetry gains power when it's spoken."

Angela cleared her throat. "For the flip side of that bounce and uncontainable joy, you have 'Tears of a Clown.' Anybody in here been forced to fall out of love before you were ready? That's a song about putting on a brave face, pretending you are absolutely okay for the whole world, but when you're alone, the tears fall, the hurt shows.

It's meaningful and it lasts. Great choice, Jason."

For too long, she watched him absorb the fact that he'd given an honest answer and she'd agreed. When she realized the silence was stretching, she clicked the remote. "And we're moving on. If any of you are song-writers, I'd suggest talking with Dr. Li. She's the best guitar player I've heard, and she loves to talk about what she knows. Here we go. Somebody mentioned Shakespeare's sonnets, an excellent example of working within the constraints of poetic form, in this case line length, rhyme scheme and a set number of syllables for each line. That's a lot of rules, but there's a power in that control."

She pointed up at the screen. "Like I said, this class is easy. Experience the thrill and terror of having your best efforts read and discussed in public. As simple as that. Today we're going to dissect some images written by poets who aren't here to bleed from the tiny cuts of our critique. We'll start critiques on Monday, so this week, I need a poem from everyone in this class, because that's the reason we're here. My grading is a single check mark. Yes, you turned something in on time. Check."

One quick survey of each student's face revealed what she'd come to expect. Some of them trusted her. Some of them didn't. The class would shrink after the first critique session. It always did.

Nikki raised her hand again and slowly lowered it as Angela shook her head. "Are we going to read any of your poetry, Dr. Simmons?"

Now, this was interesting. No one had ever asked her that. Lots of teachers used their works as examples, but that intensified the power of criticism in Angela's experience. Students exerted themselves to find something to critique when the "expert" teacher was the subject. The bad reviews hurt worse and were almost inevitable.

"Not as examples. I could slip in one of my works in progress for critique." Angela shrugged out of her suit jacket. "Maybe if I'm bulletproof one day."

Nikki smiled at her answer.

She watched Jason Ward slip on glasses and flip open a notebook as she advanced to the next slide, which listed the requirements of the Elizabethan sonnet. Over the week, she'd race through different poetry forms and styles and end with the freedom and challenges of modern free verse.

Jason Ward would no doubt take careful notes about each.

That much she was certain of.

The anticipation she felt about his contribution made little sense. He might lack any creativity. His appearance suggested conventional rules suited him the best.

But tossing out "My Girl" in a room of tried-and-true textbook answers? She had her fingers crossed for unpredictable. In her experience, summer classes could be a grind. Many of the students didn't want to be there, so no matter how much she loved the subject matter, pulling them along was hard work.

She was already looking forward to next week. She hoped Jason's words lived up to the anticipation.

CHAPTER FOUR

AFTER A GOOD WEEK, filled with enough physical therapy, college classes and errands for his mother to keep him busy, Jason had hit the lull of Friday night. His mother was playing cards in her facility's poker tournament. She'd invited him to watch. The fact that he'd almost accepted her invitation was something he'd have to come to terms with. The lack of distraction teamed up with the complete silence made it impossible to rest.

Jason stretched out his leg and tried to ignore the throb. His last physical therapy appointment had been the stuff of legends, almost as if Terry, the five-foot-nothing trainer who'd gotten him up and walking again, was determined to prove to them both that Jason could handle whatever physical obstacles the world could toss at him. He was almost convinced the prosthesis would hold, no matter the terrain he threw at it.

Earlier, his mother had dropped him off at home in the electric-blue convertible she'd chosen to rent for a week—to test the waters, she'd said. He'd then showered away the sweat brought on by enough exercise to wear out a man with two good legs, attempted to make his own dinner and lowered himself to his favorite seat at the kitchen table to contemplate his homework.

For the past half hour, he'd stared blankly at the wall while his television, tuned to some baseball game he didn't care a thing about, provided background noise.

While he was out and about, getting home and removing his prosthesis had been his only goal, a sign to himself that he'd done something hard and could rest. Relax. There was no reason to stare up at the flat white paint on the ceiling over his bed or to flip through channel after channel on the television before giving up. He'd done everything he had to do. He should be able to settle.

No matter how hard he worked during the day, at night the restless need to move settled in. Nobody to talk to. No paperwork to finish. Since that had been the part of his job he hated the most, filling out forms to requisition items or report on deliveries made, missing it was a bad sign. For years, he'd spent so little time alone that now here he was, all by himself, and there was nothing to concentrate on but the quiet.

"You should be exhausted," he muttered to himself, irritated all over again at how difficult it was to fall asleep. For most of his life, he'd been able to sleep in whatever fits and starts were available to him. Now? There were long, beautiful stretches of uninterrupted time when he could sleep, but all he did was lie awake, getting madder and madder at himself and the smooth, boring white ceiling he was looking at, until he was forced to get up.

None of it made sense, not the insomnia or the anger.

As Jason scrolled through the poetry website on the Poet's syllabus, he scanned the titles. "Professor Simmons" was stuffy. "Dr. Simmons" was worse. In his head, "Angela" worked but "the Poet" was safer. He admired her cleverness. If she'd mentioned she was the teacher at registration, would he have signed up?

Angela Simmons was good at her job. The students sitting in a circle had started to follow her steps around the classroom the way a flower turns toward the sun. She was captivating when she lectured, likely because she loved it. That was easy to see. If he was being honest, ever since her first glowing approval of his Smokey answer, he'd weighed every comment he made. He wanted the same glow every time she responded to him. After watching her talk so passionately about poetry for a week, he had a bad feeling he hadn't outgrown having a crush on his professor.

He had definitely aged out of homework, though, and now he was up against a deadline.

He'd hoped reading poetry would inspire writing it.

And his standards had risen. At the beginning, he'd expected to muddle through.

Now he wanted to impress the Poet. He scanned the poem titles on the website. "So much love. So little war," he muttered. No matter how hard he tried, he could not come up with a subject fit to trot out in front of his classmates, much less the woman he'd spent too much time thinking about outside of the classroom. What would they write about? Love, the most popular topic. College freshmen and sophomores would still have confidence in love.

But his images were the opposite—fire and explosions—and entirely too much for innocent college kids from south Florida.

The Poet had shown them all kinds of works. Not one of them had included midnight raids or the ringing in his ears after a bomb had gone off.

"Nature. You could write about the beach or flowers or other simple things." He stretched back to study the smooth paint, this time on his dining room ceiling, and heard the faintest shout of laughter. The timing was suspicious, as if his own conscience was amused at the idea of him stringing together a collection of words to pay homage to crashing waves. When it happened again, he decided he was listening to real laughter. Somewhere, there were real people enjoying themselves. Obviously, they were not trying to write poetry.

Jason checked the time on his laptop. Almost midnight. Somewhere close by, there were people who were also not sleeping, and, while they were not sleeping, they were happy-ish, instead of trying to chase very real memories away with weak poetic images.

He wasn't dressed to go out and make new friends. He'd left off the prosthesis to give his skin time to breathe. All the walking he'd done on the treadmill—uphill and then with differing speeds—while Terry barked "Faster" in his face had irritated the skin as much as it had annoyed him.

He didn't want to put it back on. Not tonight. And he didn't want to drag jeans on, pin up the leg to prevent tripping himself on crutches. He couldn't see the sense in going through all that hassle just to have company that would distract him when he should be sleeping.

It was late.

Staying right here was the smart choice. Right?

Jason smoothed a hand over the red skin on his knee. The scars weren't so bad, but he didn't go out in public with them on display. He didn't want to be a spectacle or deal with the attention that lit a fire under his simmering anger.

He'd always been in control. Until now.

One of the memories that kept floating back to the top while he tried to rest was of a parade in Rosette. He'd been five or six. Hopped up on sugar and running wild with the pack that always followed him, he'd nearly tripped a Vietnam vet walking the parade route. His mother had been able to yank him out of way of being swatted. The man moved slowly but swung his cane like a baseball bat. The anger—that was the part that stuck with Jason.

He'd never been able to understand it.

Until now.

He shook his head. "Lost some of your guts along with your foot, Ward." After yanking his crutch closer, Jason stood and went to his bedroom. He pulled on a clean T-shirt. Shorts and a crutch would be fine. It was dark. How much would people see anyway? "Bunch of vets in this place. No one is going to be traumatized by your leg."

In the two weeks he'd been at Concord Court, he'd met zero of his neighbors.

Chalk that up to the fact that he was always either at school, the medical center for rehab or inside his apartment. Unless they broke in and sat on the couch his mother had insisted on buying him, Jason would never meet his neighbors.

Unless a midnight walk was the right situation.

"You'll never know if you mope at your kitchen table as if you're scared." The jeans he'd worn to his PT appointment were draped over the dirty-clothes hamper. Mad at himself, Jason tossed the shorts aside, plucked up the jeans and then went to sit on the side of his bed. Attaching his prosthesis burned as he'd expected it would, but it was becoming familiar. He'd finally mastered fitting the umbrella close enough before rolling on the liner. Jason attached his leg and eased to stand carefully while he waited for the pin to snap in place. "Oh, good."

In the early days, he'd been sure he'd never get the hang of putting on and taking off his leg.

After Jason tugged on his jeans, he stood carefully, settled his weight and then walked toward the front door. His shoes were in a short, neat line; he stepped into the running shoes that hadn't seen any running lately and studied the smooth surface of the door.

He could do this. Over the course of a military career, he'd introduced himself to new groups countless times. Why was opening this door as traumatizing as the first day of kindergarten?

Jason eased the door open and paused. Maybe he wouldn't hear the laughter again. He could go back inside and do more memorizing of the ceiling paint in his new, comfortable home. He was already excelling at the "not writing poetry" goal.

A low murmur of conversation drifted by. "The pool." That was the direction the noise had come from. Whether he was right or wrong, it was a perfectly normal destination for a stroll at midnight if a man couldn't sleep. He could say he wanted to check out the foliage around the gated area in the bright light of the moon. Bougainvillea. Hibiscus. He even knew the lingo already.

He was on the verge of poetry while he drafted his solid excuse to walk where he wanted to walk even if the cool kids didn't approve, but Jason shook his head and headed down the pathway to the pool area.

As he turned the bend in the path, the conversation grew steadier, easier to understand, even if he couldn't make out every word. Instead of intentionally softening his step for stealth, Jason kept up a steady pace even after the noise died down. As he expected, everyone involved in the poolside conversation had turned to watch his approach as he made it to the wrought iron gate that gave the place such a high-end appearance.

"Evening." He slowed, ready to retreat with his almost reasonable excuse at the first impression that they didn't want his company. In the darkness, he could count three guys and one petite woman settled at a table in the corner of the paved patio. A battery-operated lantern in the center of the table was the only direct light in their shadowed area.

"Couldn't sleep?" one of the men asked before he motioned with one hand at an empty chair. "Us, either. Occupational hazard."

As Jason fumbled with the latch on the gate, somebody turned up the glow from the lantern. The woman added, "Since the pool is closed at this hour and we're not technically supposed to be out here, we try to keep a low profile."

Jason moved carefully around the landscaping before easing down into the empty seat at the table.

"Boss isn't here tonight. She had to go to some fund-raiser, so she's staying at her father's villa in Gables Estates," the guy next to Jason said before he extended his hand. "Sean Wakefield. Handyman, on-call security, interim assistant manager and all-around favorite here at Concord Court. I was wondering when you'd join us."

Jason shook his hand. "Is there a joining requirement? An initiation ceremony or something?" He stretched to shake the other hands offered around the table and noticed a dark, dog-shaped blob spread out at the bottom of the railing.

"That's Bo. Dogs are not technically allowed by the pool, either. He's in training to be a service animal. Need one?" Sean asked.

"A dog? No. Thanks, but I'll meet Bo when he wakes up from his nap," Jason said as he tried to place Sean's drawl. "Is that Georgia I hear?"

"Yep. You, too?" Sean asked.

"Yeah, near Atlanta." Jason was surprised how nice it was to find that touch of home. In the army, he'd listened to accents from all over the world, and that drawl had lost some of its unique flavor. Here, it reminded him of fishing with his dad and a half dozen different football coaches.

"I was born with one toe on the Alabama line," Sean said. "This is Marcus Bryant, Peter Kim, also known as Anchor because he's the only one around here with a boat, and the little lady is Mira Peters." The faint grumble that followed his introduction suggested the little lady didn't appreciate his description.

"This little lady hits hard as a man, jarhead." The words were brisk, but she didn't move an inch.

"It was a term of respect, Mira, not an insult." Sean's drawl was thick. Too thick even for a Georgia boy. "Ain't nobody here need you to prove how tough you are. Running with you is a pure misery, and I do not know why I do it."

"I do. It's because you're afraid I'll drag you out of bed if you don't show up in the morning. You hate running with me when

I'm in a good mood. Imagine how much worse it is when I'm mad. Nobody likes a quitter." She drawled to match his.

Was this an argument they had often?

Jason waited for the flurry of trash talk to die down. "Occupational hazard, you said. Where do you work?"

Marcus answered, "He meant our previous occupation. Most of us were air force, although we have one proud marine. You?"

"Army." Jason realized he didn't have to tell them anything more. He didn't have to explain what kind of work he'd done or where he'd been. Civilians often followed up the first question, the one about which branch he'd served in, with another getting-to-know-you request in order to fill in the awkward silence that could bloom. Before his injury, he'd struggled to answer those questions. No matter how much people appreciated his service, there was an awkwardness because they didn't understand a thing about it. He'd never come up with a good way to get through that. Leaving the conversation had been his best maneuver.

"Good to meet you, Ward. Don't call me Anchor. Yes, I have a boat. No, you can't use it." Peter reached behind him. The rustling ice followed by a snap told Jason a drink was headed his way. A cold bottle touched his hand as Peter said, "Have a drink. That's the only initiation ceremony we need except for serving your country in some place you never want to see again, not even in your dreams."

Not even in his dreams. Yeah. That was right.

Jason turned the bottle slowly in his hand. Not even in his dreams. If he were a real poet, there might be something to that arrangement of words. It spoke to him. If he were a poet, he might be able to expand them so that other people could understand them, too.

"So, you got a work detail?" Sean asked as if he hardly cared.

"No job yet. Decided to give school a shot. For my mother." Mama's boy. So what? She was all he had. He waited for the grief they were going to heap on his head.

The chorus of sighs that answered convinced him they understood how mothers could get things done.

"Yeah, I get that. You going to Sawgrass?"

Mira asked. "I enrolled last fall. Got three more semesters before I can finally finish my Bachelor of Science."

"Then what?" Marcus asked. "Nursing school?"

Her grumble was closer to a growl. "Because I'm a woman?"

He cleared his throat. "Because you were a medic. I should have asked about medical school. That's what I meant anyway."

In the dark and wide-open air of the outdoor pool area, tension should have been difficult to feel, but Jason was sure every man at the table had the uneasy sensation that violence was imminent. That prickle of sensation indicated something bad was coming. The first time he was deployed, somebody called it an itch, that restless itch that meant he better pay close attention because he was going to be forced to move out fast.

Instead, Mira let out a long, soft sigh. "No. No hospitals for me. I'm lucky to be here as it is. I'm going to be a teacher. Junior high. I'm going to dissect earthworms or teach the periodic table or the layers of the earth's core or something that keeps me in a classroom. That's all I ever wanted. Ever."

They were quiet. Jason wasn't sure why everyone else was silent. He understood how joining the military was one thing in a person's head and a completely different animal in real life, a dream that twisted into a nightmare. It was a life-and-death difference for some people. A medic who'd been deployed to save lives in the desert would have lived through the worst war had to offer. Who could ever sign up for that even if she'd dreamed of being a doctor?

"My mother wants me to become an accountant." Jason threw it out there, hoping it would lighten the mood. The pause followed by snickers around the table convinced him he might have found a few people who knew exactly where he was coming from. "And teaching has gotta be safer than patrols outside of Kandahar."

"I don't know, man. Junior high was hard in my day. Today it's twice as dangerous." Marcus, the guy who'd put his boot in his mouth with the nursing school crack, sounded thoughtful. "Teachers do not get paid enough."

"And neither do soldiers." Peter raised his bottle. "To that, we drink." At the loud clink of glass bottles, he said in a low growl, "We drink quietly."

"You said Reyna isn't here tonight." Mira turned down the lantern.

"She knows everything that happens here." Sean cleared his throat. "And she signs my paycheck, so I try to be a little more…"

"Obedient? Well trained?" Marcus drawled. "Like your dogs?"

There was no grumble, but Sean set his bottle down. "Definitely, although my dogs have excellent manners and I am known to pee on the furniture now and then."

The muffled chuckles around the table eased some of the tension in Jason's shoulders. It was good to talk to people who knew exactly what he'd been through. They might have served in a different part of the world with a different job and a completely different threat, but they knew about military life and the loneliness and the fear that was hard to shake even in the safe and familiar quarters of south Florida's comfortable Concord Court.

"Accounting, huh? Taking your first class this summer?" Mira asked.

Jason squeezed his eyes shut. "Actually, I decided to try creative writing instead."

The silence around the table was the calm before the storm. He knew that much.

"How very 'teen rebellion' of you. Are you making up for lost time?" There was a thread of amusement in Sean's voice.

Jason cleared his throat. "I wanted something easy. Someone told me it was the easiest class on campus. My plan was to take a class to show my mother I could do it and get on with my life. Whatever that is."

He stretched out his leg and tipped his head back to study the sky. Light pollution and cloud cover hid most of the stars, but it was nice to listen to muffled city noise and know that he wasn't alone.

"How's that working out for you? Taking the easy road always sounds so good in theory. Then you give it a shot and figure out it only looked easy because all the hard parts were hidden away." From Mira's tone, Jason had a pretty good idea she knew what she was talking about. If he had to guess, that deep knowledge about how tricky the easy road could be was tied directly to her own discovery that being a medic was a world away from what she wanted for her life.

"Yeah. It's working so well that I was supposed to be writing a poem tonight. Instead, here I am." Jason sighed. "Easy class. Turn in the work. That's all I have to do, and I'm going to miss my first deadline."

Jason tangled his fingers together over his stomach and closed his eyes. It was so peaceful here he wondered if this might be the key to curing his insomnia. Sleeping outside. He'd done it before but not by choice. At least he wouldn't end up with sand stuck to his face. He hated sand.

"Poetry. I can help you with that." Sean tapped Jason's shoulder. "Roses are red. Violets are blue. Bo's ears are floppy, and so is his tail." He took a victorious swig of his beer.

"That doesn't even rhyme." Mira shook with laughter, but she kept it under control.

"Not all poetry has to rhyme. Isn't that right, Ward?" Sean said. "He knows. The man's a student."

"That's right, but it does have to make sense. What does a floppy tail mean? I guess they're all floppy?" Jason stared harder at the dark, dog-shaped shadow that had not stirred while they'd been seated around the table.

"He's asleep. His whole body is floppy right now. It makes sense." Sean tapped his bottle to Jason's. "You're free to use that. No charge."

Jason tried to imagine the Poet's face if he turned in Sean's poem. The first time they'd met, she'd been wholesome. Perfect. As if a spark of light glowed from the inside. He'd been the exact opposite, half a second from ruining the peace with his mother.

But when he'd watched her lecture about the iambic foot and rhyme schemes and the world of possibilities of blank verse or free verse, he'd seen that spark transition into something magnetic. Instead of a model-perfect collegiate professor, she'd been active and passionate about bending the rules to reinvent them.

Jason didn't bend rules, but he wanted to.

When someone loved something as much as she did teaching her class, a man had the urge to step up his game.

Unfortunately, he had no poetry game. Zero. Less than zero.

"I may have to use your floppy tail. The only images I can come up with—" Jason stared up at the dark sky again "—aren't poetic."

"Right," Mira softly agreed, "but they are truth."

Jason sipped his beer as he considered that. Truth. That was what Angela's whole focus had been in that first class. How writing and poets can take their own truth and make it universal. Jason traced his thumb over the label on the bottle. He should have asked her how that worked when the truth was better covered up instead of exposed.

The truth about nightmares was that nothing stopped, nothing cut through and nothing changed. Every night, he relived explosions and pain and heat and fear. Why would anyone want to put that on paper for other people?

Love and romance and hope. Those things had value.

But it was harder to understand the value of the story he had to tell.

"Roses are red, violets are blue, candy is sweet, and so is honey." Sean propped his feet up on the table. "I could do this all night. Want to grab a pen and paper to write some of these down?"

The laughter that followed eased some of the worry that this was going to be the way he felt for the rest of his life.

In every squad or platoon or group, people had their roles. There was the leader, the one who could inspire others to follow the hardest orders. Jason had always assumed that role, whether he meant to or not. There was the mother hen, the one who watched over the weakest or the ones weak in the moment. Sometimes you might find one who was the troublemaker or the fighter.

But the guy every group needed? Mr. Comic Relief. They kept spirits up when everything was lost.

Even if they had to spout bad poetry.

"You have a knack for this, Wakefield. Ever thought about enrolling in a class to hone the talent?" Mira asked, shaking with laughter again.

"Nah. Too many irons in the fire. This place would fall down without me. Bo's got all of his little quirks still to be ironed out and I've already promised him to an old soldier up in Tampa. My clock is ticking, you know?" Even in the dark, Jason could see that his boot didn't twitch. For a man with all these responsibilities, he sure relaxed as if he had nothing but time. If the clock was ticking, it wasn't loud. "Tomorrow, when the sun's up, we work. Tonight, we recover. Even Reyna's gotta give us time for that." He raised his bottle for a toast.

After they'd clinked bottles, Jason asked, "What's her story? I'm guessing officer of some kind."

"You asked her out, didn't you?" Sean said before he whistled. The others at the table immediately shushed him. "I wish I'd seen that. I get to watch sometimes. New guys come in, give it a shot. The answer is always no, but sometimes it ends badly. You'd be shocked at how often a man can't take no for an answer."

"I didn't ask her out. Never even crossed my mind." It hadn't. Why was that? He'd never had a problem talking to women. Getting a yes to an invitation was a matter of odds. If one lady said no, odds were the next one would say yes. For some reason, the flash of a pretty brunette's face sparkling as she made broad gestures regarding the Beat poets flashed through his mind.

That was disturbing.

Beat poets should not be taking up valuable real estate in his head.

The Poet shouldn't either, for that matter. It would be a long time before he'd have anything to offer her.

"Reyna doesn't do fun. She suspects you men might want to take her out where she'll be forced to enjoy her life. She doesn't do that." Sean cleared his throat. "And she doesn't approve of people who do. She's about service and duty and sucking the joy out of sunny days."

"And about helping people who need it and being the best and a thousand other fine qualities. Plus, she's beautiful, you ingrate," Mira snapped. "This place runs as well as it does because of her."

That tension lit up the air again. Eventually, Sean mumbled, "You're right. She's amazing. She doesn't have time for the likes of us." He tipped back his bottle.

"Ignore him," Mira said. "Reyna's great. She's focused on goals, and men are not goals. Plenty of other fish at Sawgrass."

The Poet's face was there again, her gleaming eyes hard to forget. When Jason imagined turning in something he'd written, a hard knot formed in his stomach. If he turned in a "roses are red" poem, he'd never recover his footing with her.

Tomorrow. Sean was right. Tomorrow was for work. When the sun came up, he'd write something better than a floppy tail.

And if he couldn't, at the very least, he could rhyme something with blue.

Tomorrow he'd work.

Tonight was about recovery. For the first time since he'd arrived at Concord Court, he was beginning to understand how lucky he was to have found it.

Other places would have plain townhomes and nice pools.

No other place that he knew of would have a therapy group that took place at midnight, with icy cold beer, next to the deserted pool.

CHAPTER FIVE

ON SATURDAY MORNING, Angela searched around her house for something to hold her interest. Coping with her daughter's absence was easier during the busier spring and fall semesters. As head of the English department, Angela taught a couple of classes and had all the departmental oversight work to keep herself busy. But during this summer semester there was nothing to grade, and preparation for the fall semester wouldn't kick into high gear for another month. Angela was adjusting to the realization that Greer wouldn't be coming to stay for the summer, and she wasn't taking it as well as she'd hoped.

She could tell because she was stretched out on her daughter's bed, both legs dangling over the wooden footboard and her head propped up on a fuzzy hot pink pillow, while she talked to Greer on the phone. "And what did you do on Wednesday?"

The silence on the other end of the call made her wonder if Greer had gotten bored and moved on. Then her daughter said carefully, "Do you need an hourly play-by-play, Mom? We talked on Wednesday. I told you how it was going on Wednesday. There were phone calls. I shadowed the senator's chief of staff in a committee meeting. We don't have to go over it again, do we?"

Angela wrinkled her nose. She'd be happy to go over it all again, but Greer was smart. "No. I'm thrilled you're enjoying the internship, though. It's funny how excited you are about making photocopies. If I'd known that was all it took to satisfy you, I could have put you to work in my office." Angela stared up at her toes and wondered if a pedicure would improve her mood. It definitely couldn't hurt.

"I wish you had exciting stories to tell me, even if they were about office machinery. Creative writing should be a rich source of gossip, but no." Greer had her father's dry sense of humor. It was one of the things Angela had loved about him in the early days, and hearing it provoked a homesick pang. Not for him. Not even really for Nashville, but just this, the daily "we're a family" time.

"We're going to start the critiques next week. Poetry. I'm excited." Angela had already logged in every poem and done a quick read. There had been a few surprising gems, and she expected the comments to be fun.

The one she'd been most excited to read? Yeah. Missing. No assignment from Jason Ward. That had been when her mood had taken a nosedive on Friday and she had yet to recover.

There was no good reason for the anticipation she'd tried to squash all week, and the funk she was in because he hadn't completed the assignment was all out of proportion. She'd have a good class with or without Jason Ward's writing. Some of the pieces she'd read were strong right out of the gate. Those students would only improve. This class was right on track compared with all the others she'd taught.

After she'd closed up her class file for the week and answered the two emails that had come in on Friday, Angela had returned to her comfortable, empty bungalow and spent entirely too much time scrolling through happy pictures and posts from her friends, family and her ex. Instead of excitement over a beautiful weekend, she was experiencing heavy fear of missing out and annoying her daughter because of it.

"Got big plans for the day?" she asked, determined not to be weird. No matter what Angela did, Greer would think she was strange in a Mom way, but she was going to get a grip before truly odd behavior kicked in. The urge to go to Nashville was growing, but she had no chance to go and the reason… Well, being caught up in the aura of the happy glow had to be worse in person than over the internet.

"Dad and Kate are going baby furniture shopping this weekend, and I said I'd go, too. They're planning to have lunch at Frederico's, and you know I love that place." Greer's rushed words might as well have been a guilty confession. "I hardly ever go there since you moved away."

The last time they'd spread out in a shadowy booth together at Frederico's, Angela had still been married, Greer had gotten her braces off and homemade lasagna had been on both their minds.

"Frederico's. I miss that place." Angela knew Greer needed to get off the phone. She had plenty of options for her Saturday, but Angela didn't want to end the call. "The colors Kate has picked out are pretty neutral. Are they going to find out whether it's a boy or girl?" Angela asked in the most normal, upbeat voice she could manage.

"Depends on the day. Right now, they're on the 'what a fun surprise it will be to find out when the baby arrives' train. Oh, and Dad's sports obsession is taking over. He can't decide whether the baby will be playing football or soccer in high school." Greer huffed a breath. "You know he's been hoping for an athlete since I tripped over grass blades on every field I ever stepped on."

"We never did find a team that valued falling down, did we?" Angela pictured her ex plotting the next twenty athletic years. There was a whiteboard and spreadsheets involved, which Angela loved. Unfortunately, that was the only thing that he enjoyed planning. Tournaments. Fantasy leagues. Meanwhile, when Greer was born, Angela had immediately drawn up a savings plan with the Ivy League in mind.

At least Rodney's willingness to follow her plans was a good thing. Greer had her goals. Thanks to Angela, she and Rodney could support those without a worry. Both of them had saved, and now both of them could live comfortable lives.

"I hope you aren't spending too much time watching all this, Mom. You know how it is. In their little bubble, things are great, but life goes on for everyone else. Traffic on the interstate is terrible because who knows why everything gets so backed up, but it takes almost forty-five minutes to get to and from the Capitol. Dad's road rage is under control but still way too much for eight o'clock in the morning. Kate is throwing up. A lot. We have to have dinner at six o'clock on the dot or nausea takes her out. None of that makes it into the daily glowing reports, you know? If you only read their posts, it's all registries and gifts and giggles."

Giggles. Was that a clue about how Greer felt? It wasn't a normal Greer word and certainly not an activity her brainy daughter would envy.

Angela tilted her head back and stared at the hot pink rose wallpaper Greer had convinced her to put up when she'd stayed last summer. Angela had expected to hate it. She'd expected her daughter to hate it before she'd gone home, but it had grown on her. Greer made smart decisions.

And she gave good advice.

"What a smart kid you are. That's a good reminder. I am not wasting time on their posts." Not much. Not anymore, if she could get a handle on the urge. "I get all my news from you, the way it should be." Such a big lie to slip right off the tongue. Every day at lunchtime, Angela logged on to read updates. "I love my class. I'm planning meetings with my department to get the fall semester set. And today I'm going to the beach. My life is full."

As soon as she said it, Angela closed her eyes. She hated beaches. There was too much sand. It was everywhere. And the heat.

But if Nashville had Greer and weddings and babies and old friends, Miami had beaches. Lots of people loved beaches. She would go to one of the famous ones. Miami Beach or South Beach. She would post her own photos of the sand and water and beautiful people, and her friends in Nashville could feel sorry for themselves that they had no beach.

Perfect.

Sometimes she stumbled onto the answer without trying, like Greer had stumbled over perfectly flat soccer fields once upon a time.

"A beach. That's great." Greer's pause warned Angela that she was about ten seconds from mentioning that Angela was not a beach person.

"I won a free tour of Millionaire's Row. I'm going to go gawk at how the other half lives. On a boat." There. That had a touch of enthusiasm. She hadn't won a tour, but she knew where to buy a ticket. "While I'm there, I'm going to do some touristy shopping and grab ice cream at that place we went to, the one that mixes all the ingredients you want right into the ice cream." There. The ice cream would add a touch of truth to the whole thing. There was one thing she never passed up and it was cold and creamy.

She and Greer had discovered the place when she'd come for a quick visit at Christmas.

"I loved that ice cream. The next time we go, I'm going to skip the sprinkles and go straight for chocolate chips. All the chocolate chips," Greer said. Her daughter had been a chocoholic from day one and hearing her say that brought back memories of their summer together in Miami and about a hundred other times she'd ended up with chocolate smeared on her lips as a girl. How much of Greer was she missing down here?

"I guess I better go so I don't miss my tour, and you need to work up an appetite for Frederico's. I love you, Greer. I miss you, but I am so proud of you, baby." *No tears. Do not let the tears out.*

"I miss you, too, but I'll be your shadow at the wedding, follow you everywhere."

"Any news on their plans?" Angela asked, aiming for disinterested. That was the goal. She still had her fingers crossed that her invitation would get lost in the mail.

"Yesterday, while Dad and I were cleaning up the kitchen after dinner, he said they were hunting for places in Key West. Kate wants something sunny. Dad wants upscale. Wouldn't that be awesome? We never made it down there, and I still want to pet the six-toed cats and touch the southernmost point. When I mentioned the cats, Dad started and will not shut up about Hemingway and Frost and blah-blah-blah. They have to find a venue at the last minute, so it isn't easy. Everywhere they call is booked, but if they make this work, I'll either come early to stay for a week with you or stay after until school starts. What do you think?"

"Awesome. I can't wait." Angela shook her head. Engaged in Paris. Married in Key West. Baby on the way. Rodney was truly living his best life.

But she was going to hug Greer soon. That was something to look forward to.

"You know, it would help if you'd post some pictures of your own, Mom. This tour? Could be fun. Live a little. I want to envy your ice cream, and don't forget the choco-late chips." Greer's bossy voice was back. That was a good sign. "I worry about you down there by yourself."

At that, Angela wrinkled her nose. Who was the mother here?

"Got it. Love you. Call me tomorrow sometime and tell me about Frederico's."

Angela draped an arm over her face as she dropped the phone beside her head.

By herself. That was Greer's concern.

All Angela could do was prove there were advantages to independence.

And now she had no choice. She'd told Greer she was going out. If she didn't have photographic evidence to back up her claims, her daughter would never let her live it down.

After an awkward attempt to roll smoothly off the bed, Angela picked up the pillows she'd knocked to the floor and straightened the lampshade. The best part of living alone was the lack of an audience for her occasional awkwardness. She would say Greer had inherited her lack of grace, after all, Angela hadn't had a lot to start with. Still, dancing in the kitchen to Smokey Robinson while she washed the dishes was allowed here. There was no teenage daughter to die of embarrassment.

The increased rotation of Motown hits in her house could be traced back to Jason Ward. Even if he never turned in anything, she'd have that to thank him for.

"Get out of the house before you let that

reminder depress you again," Angela muttered to herself. After a quick brush of her hair into a ponytail and a swipe of mascara and lip gloss, Angela slipped on her sandals, grabbed her keys and purse, and slid behind the wheel of her sedan. "Too bad you are not a convertible." The not-a-convertible but perfectly reliable car started smoothly and in a minute she was zipping down the freeway toward Miami Beach.

"A parking spot at a tourist trap—Miami's true pot of gold," Angela murmured as she rolled slowly through the parking deck. Spying a truck backing out of a spot in fits and starts, Angela accelerated and managed to nab the spot before a minivan with Tennessee plates got there. "Too bad, Tennessee. Sometimes the locals win."

Was she a local? Not really. But all of her bills were delivered to a Florida address, so she could make the claim here and now. Once she'd conquered the parking challenge, it was as easy as the fresh breeze whipping through the outdoor kiosks lining the waterfront to find the tour she wanted. One quick swipe of her credit card, and she was ready to board.

"How many in your party, miss?" the kid taking tickets asked.

Before she could decide about how she felt about his "miss," she said, "One. Just me."

His hesitation suggested that wasn't the usual, but he motioned her forward, and she quickly forgot the tiny pinch of the reminder that she was single in a world meant for couples because she was on a boat. Sand was terrible. Deep, dark water like the ocean wasn't her favorite. Spending time on a boat? Refreshing and exciting and fun. Angela claimed a seat near the rear of the boat and settled in to be wowed.

After more than an hour of craning her neck to gape at the places where actors, musicians, gangsters and everyday multimillionaires lived, she had plenty of pictures to post and a sunburn on her nose, and she'd dumped a whole lot of stress right into the bay.

"Watch your step." The captain of the ship was standing on the dock as Angela stepped down. He was wearing the crisp white uniform, the hat, the whole captain ensemble. This was an excellent selfie opportunity. She was behind in the selfie game, but it was impossible to miss this chance. "Thank you for joining us." He offered her his hand. "And if there's anything we can do to make your visit to Miami better, please do let us know." Instead of letting go, he held her hand and Angela froze.

"Oh, I'm not visiting. I live here." Why did she have to correct that? Was he hitting on her? Right out here in the open? In front of people?

When she managed to meet his stare, he smiled slowly. He was. Oh boy. When she told Greer, her girl was going to freak. And then she decided to go for it.

"Captain, would you…" She wasn't going to do it.

Was she?

"Could we take a selfie together?" Angela shrugged. "That would be a great souvenir for this day."

He took her phone from her before draping an arm over her shoulder in a friendly manner. "Say cheese, then."

Stunned at her own boldness, Angela tilted her chin up and gave the biggest grin she could muster. Ready to hurry back to the boardwalk so she could post the photo and wait for Greer's call, Angela held out her hand but the captain was… Was he entering his phone number? Oh man.

"In case you might like to get together sometime, Miss I-live-here."

The urge to deny that she may be interested was strong. But she smiled and said, "Thanks for the photo and the tour." Angela desperately hoped he missed the flush of… what? Embarrassment? It would be best if he assumed she'd gotten too much sun.

In a hurry to escape now, Angela forced her feet into what she remembered walking looked like. When she made it to the end of the dock, she refused to check over her shoulder.

Since the divorce, she'd focused on rebuilding her life and work. Not men.

Did she want to spend any time tangled up with dating now? Hard to say.

"Ice cream. That will fix everything." The nervous flutter in her stomach was unusual. It had been so long since she'd been in that situation. Her body was fighting off its own freak-out.

"You need a captain." When she realized what she'd said, Angela said slowly, "Caption. Not captain. Caption." Talking to herself out loud while she waited for her turn to build her own ice cream was worrisome, so Angela bit her lip and concentrated on what the *caption* might be. Nothing was coming to mind. Having a man get her number had rattled all the creativity away.

She'd met Rodney in college. They'd married as soon as he graduated, and then they'd been together until almost three years ago. After the separation, while they tried to work out how to stay together, and after the divorce that blew apart her life and relocating to Miami, men were not even on the list of things to do.

But that zing of awareness? She'd missed it. In a hurry, she typed, Is this the Love Boat? under the photo and posted it. Then she shoved her phone back in her pocket.

"Here you are, miss." The teen girl behind the counter couldn't be any older than Greer, but she'd still gone with "miss" instead of "ma'am." Angela should stick with a ponytail and sunglasses every day. Without them, she never failed to be called "ma'am."

Angela snapped a picture of her ice-cream cone, took the cone and the bottle of water, and then stepped back out on the boardwalk. She'd stroll and eat her dessert, then go find seafood. When she posted those photos, she'd need something clever to say about them. Angela licked her ice cream and poked the empty spot in her brain where good words should be. With a shrug, she studied the boardwalk. The words would come.

She was a writer. This was her thing.

As she walked along and idly studied the windows of the souvenir shops and the kiosks selling airboat rides, haunted after-dark tours and enough T-shirts for everyone in Florida, Angela turned the corner to the quieter end of the boardwalk. The parking deck was to the right, but she wasn't quite ready to go home, so she went left. From this shady end, she could see the bustle of the tours, the swimming area on the opposite side of the bay and the marina that stretched for miles past the parking garage.

And there, on a bench, was Jason Ward.

This was a tourist trap. She hadn't expected to run into any of her students or Sawgrass faculty.

She certainly wasn't dressed to impress

with scholarly authority. The ponytail and sunglasses were drawing *miss*es instead of *ma'am*s.

If she hadn't frozen in her tracks, she might have had the opportunity to skulk away if she'd wanted to. Since Angela couldn't decide what she wanted—to escape without notice or to engage in a conversation with the student who had such interesting things to say—it was fine that fate took the choice out of her hands.

Jason turned and looked right at her. "Is this one of those places where, if I sit here long enough, the whole world walks by?" Jason made a show of studying the lack of foot traffic. "Can't be that, so do you come here often?" He frowned, as if that wasn't his best effort.

Since she was struggling to come up with witty one-liners herself that afternoon, Angela understood.

And it was enough to put her at ease. "I come here never. You must live here on this bench."

Jason shook his head. "Never seen it before in my life. It's almost as if we were meant to run into each other today. No other way to explain it, is there?"

Angela considered that. "I guess not, and I did need to talk with you. About your assignment, the one I don't have."

He sighed long and loud. "I should have let you keep on walking. You were going to move right on past me as if you didn't recognize me."

"But this is so much better." Angela slid down on the bench next to him. The whole day had been unexpected. She'd started something with her lie-turned-truth with Greer and it had been an adventure so far. Jason might be right. If he was meant to be a part of her adventure, he'd chosen exactly the right bench. The breathless shock of the captain and his phone number maneuver was back, but this time, when she was faced with another conversation with Jason Ward, she would definitely call the emotion excitement. There was no edge of anxiety with it, only the fizz of interest he sparked. Sunshine. The ocean. Ice cream. Yachts as far as the eye could see. And a handsome man she was going to talk to about poetry. It was nearly the perfect Saturday.

CHAPTER SIX

THERE WAS VERY little that could convince a man he'd aged overnight as well as limping around a tourist trap in search of a comfortable bench. When Jason had discovered his spot, the deserted bench in a shady bend of the boardwalk where he could watch the busy bay without all the conversation and loud, excited shouts of sugared-up kids washing over him, he'd sunk down gratefully.

Then he'd started to think.

About how his life had changed.

And if it would always be this way.

Depressing.

Realizing he wasn't alone hadn't done much to poke holes in the gloom, but when he'd turned his head to find a pretty woman with an ice-cream cone in one hand and a bottle of water in the other, he'd perked up.

The fact that she was shifting from one

foot to the other, as if she was trying to decide whether to move toward him or away, was a problem, but he'd recognized her quickly, and his mission was clear. Convincing her to move forward was easy enough. Calling her out had stopped her thoughts of retreat and now, here his creative writing professor was, seated next to him on the world's most perfect bench.

Depression disappeared in the face of anticipation. That same buzz he'd enjoyed all week. "Where did you find this?" He tapped the water bottle.

"Ice-cream parlor." She waved her cone. "I wasn't sure how long I was staying, worried I might need hydration." She held it out to him. "Thirsty? I got it for you."

He waved it off. "Thank you. Can't take it." Even if he was as thirsty as he'd ever been—like after a day run in Afghanistan—in that heartbeat, he couldn't take it.

"*Won't* take it." She set it on the seat between them. "Yet."

Was he thirsty? Yes. Would he allow his already banged-up pride to suffer further damage by accepting her charitable offer?

"You look thirsty." She shoved her sunglasses on top of her head and bit the edge of her ice-cream cone. "I have ice cream."

He was thirsty, but seeing her eyes changed his whole focus. At this range, she wasn't pure energy in motion as she was in front of her classroom. Instead, she was just a beautiful woman.

No professional's suit of armor, either.

Dressed in red shorts, a gray tank top with watermelons all over it, dark sunglasses, a swinging ponytail and sandals that showed off a bright red pedicure, she might be a cute college student.

Jason regretted that he knew what color she'd chosen for that pedicure. He'd spend too much time thinking about that now. He reached over to pick up the bottle to have something to do with his hands.

"Thank you for the water." His tone was closer to a grumble than real appreciation. Not very thankful, for sure. Walking to the ice-cream shop would take most people little energy and less time, but he wasn't most people. Not that afternoon. Jason took the cap off and swallowed quickly. It didn't burn, this swallowing of his pride. When he set it back down, her lips were curled. Was that satisfaction? Probably.

"You know, I had high hopes for you. You understand poetry. You got it day one. Some students do, some don't. I can teach a few of those who don't, but not everyone has the appreciation for what language can do. How it's a picture and music all rolled into phrases. I thought you were one of those." She shrugged a shoulder before popping the last bite of her cone in her mouth.

Jason rolled the cold bottle between his hands and straightened his legs. The skin on his left leg was burning, but some of the fatigue had receded, so it was easier to enjoy a sunny day by the water.

Now that the Poet was here anyway. Angela. Today, they were Jason and Angela.

"But now I'm the past tense. You've already given up on me? You haven't even read anything I've written." A second after the words left his mouth, Jason knew he'd fallen into her trap.

Angela waved a finger. "Exactly! You missed the deadline. I have received eleven poems in varying stages of goodness. I know because I marked up my ledger yesterday, the one I use to submit grades." She made a show of rolling up her nonexistent sleeve, which only drew his attention to her smooth skin. Angela tapped her naked wrist. "Today is Saturday. That comes after Friday, doesn't it?"

"End of the week. That was the deadline. Couldn't that be Saturday at midnight? Or our week starts on Mondays." Jason shook his head as he watched her cross one leg over the other so her foot could swing in annoyed little taps. Whatever she intended, he was enjoying the show and the conversation. "Can I have an extension?"

"Do you have a poem?" she replied, her dark brows arched. "Hit Send and I'll accept it. I should have been more specific, included an hour on my deadline."

"I'm working on it." He waved one hand expansively to take in the water and the marina. "Soaking up some nature and people. Inspiration is all around me even as we speak."

"Do I sense sarcasm, Mr. Ward?" Her tone was perfect for a schoolmarm controlling a wild classroom, but he was pretty sure they were both enjoying the conversation.

"A little, maybe. I've sat down at my computer more than once this week, read some great stuff on the sites you mentioned, but nothing came together. Your first class should have been about writer's block." Jason stared down at the bottle in his hands, one thumb picking at the label. "Everything I could write was too dark."

Angela didn't respond immediately. Eventually, she said, "My usual answer to something like that is that darkness is part of the human experience. We've all been there. We'll all be there again someday. There is truth in the hard things, maybe more than the easy, but I understand. As writers, we make the decision about what we can show other people. There are pieces of ourselves that we protect because we have to."

They were quiet, seated there on the perfect bench, while they contemplated hidden fragility.

"Do you have truth that's too hard to put into words?" Jason asked. He wasn't sure why, but the small frown and how her humor faded made him wonder if they had more in common than he'd expected.

The connection would be nice, but if her

truths were scary or dangerous, he didn't want to know.

He didn't want that for her. She was energy and enthusiasm and passion. Hurt and fear had no place in her life.

Then he realized how silly that was. Hurt and fear and all those things he hated to face belonged to everyone. They were unavoidable.

Angela shrugged a shoulder. "Lately, I've been fighting against some emotions I don't want. They aren't who I should be." She leaned closer to him. "I might have a truth that could hurt others if I spend too much time airing it out. The people who love me, who want good things for me, that's the hurt I want to prevent at any cost."

An image of his mother's stubborn face flashed in his mind. If she knew the depths of his emotions, she'd be hurt. Before he could ask Angela for more details, because he sensed there was something important there in her own world, she said, "I still need a poem from you before class starts on Monday. Paint me a picture of this day, this scene. Doesn't even have to be good. Could be a greeting card sentiment, a *cheap* greeting card sentiment. Everybody starts somewhere, Mr. Ward."

"Can you call me Jason?" he asked. What was the protocol? He wanted her to use his name.

"Yes. I just…" She nodded firmly but moved to put more space between them. "Of course I can. Jason. There. Now, will you promise to get me a poem before class starts?"

"Roses are red, violets are blue, candy is sweet, and so is honey," Jason drawled to match Sean Wakefield's delivery. "That's the best I've got, and I didn't even write it."

"The rhyme was right there, literally. 'Blue' and 'too.' 'Candy is sweet and honey is, too.'" Angela slowly tilted forward on the bench, so it was difficult to see her face until she turned her head. "I did not expect that, Jason." Her reluctant laugh was gorgeous, free and too loud. "I've been teaching a long time. It takes a lot to shock me. You did it. Your poem would work, except you admitted you didn't write it. Can't let that go. Fortunately, it shouldn't be hard to write something similar." She plopped back on the bench, one hand wrapped over her stomach.

Jason would drop the class if that was the best poem he could write. "A note on the rhyme. Got it. That's why you're the teacher. I'll come up with something better. My creativity needed some fresh air." Getting outside had always worked to clear his mind. The leg had eliminated his number one remedy: running.

"So, instead of one of the many less-crowded spots in southern Florida, you're at a tourist trap in Miami Beach." Angela pursed her lips. "Interesting tactic."

Since he'd grimly muttered the same thing to himself when his mother insisted he accompany her here, he couldn't disagree.

"New in town. I need a local to show me the best spots." He stretched an arm along the bench and waited for her to turn toward him. How easy it would be to seize his chance. To ask her out. The pinch at his knee reminded him he wasn't ready to run yet.

Her quick grin convinced him she knew exactly where he was headed, but she was good at swerving. "Too bad I'm not a local. I could give you some tips, but I've only been here two years. I'm still hunting them myself."

He'd opened the door. She'd pulled it gently closed. Fair enough.

"If it's not Miami, where is home?" Jason asked. He hadn't expected them to both be fish out of water, but he liked the connection.

"Let's see. I was born in Virginia, but my daughter is in Nashville. I guess that's home. It was for a long time. When I get homesick, I miss Greer. That must be home." She looked down at his arm on the bench, but she didn't brush it away. The tip of her chin convinced him she was weighing the rights and wrongs of their conversation. It wouldn't do to let her think about it for too long.

"How old is she?" Good question. Whatever ups and downs he'd gone through, he hadn't forgotten how to keep someone talking.

"In actual years, almost seventeen. In maturity, forty or fifty. Scary smart." Angela pulled her phone from her pocket and wiped away all the messages cluttering the screen to pull up a picture. "Here we are, last summer, at a nice beach off Key Biscayne if you're ever hoping for more sand and sea than yachts and tourists."

"Sand is overrated, but the sea is nice." Jason studied the picture. Greer was a younger version of Angela. Same dark hair with a bright smile. They were messy and happy. "Why isn't she here?"

Some of Angela's pride dimmed a bit. "Greer's in a great school with big plans to make it to Harvard or Yale, where she will earn a law degree and change the world. She's working an internship that my ex finagled with a state senator and her life is right on track. I couldn't stay in Nashville, not teaching at the same university where my ex-husband would be my boss." She wrinkled her nose. "I also couldn't bear to pull her away from everything she dreamed of, so sometimes I'm homesick."

If he had to guess, they'd wandered into the neighborhood where that truth that might hurt others if Angela explored it too deeply lived, but he was the last guy to poke where it hurt. Her truth, her timeline. They were quiet, but Jason could see more notifications cascading over Greer's happy photo.

"Ever get homesick yourself?" Angela

asked. She wasn't watching him, but he had a feeling she knew a thing about deflecting tension.

"It's harder for me. I was born in Georgia. My family was there. My father is buried there. I expected the same for my mother. Instead, she's here, forcing me out on Saturday so she can cross something off her bucket list. I joined the army when I was eighteen, so I've lived in a whole lot of places."

Jason took a chance and brushed one hand over her shoulder. "Homesickness, though—I get how it can be for a person more than a place. Those bright sails over there?" He pointed with his free hand and waited for her to nod. "That's my mother. You met her at Sawgrass that first day. She's moved to Miami to be close to me and now she's determined to 'live a little.' Those are her words. As if she didn't run Rosette High School from the administration office gleefully and with a firm fist."

"She's over there? Parasailing? I'm going to try that someday." The spark of excitement in Angela's eyes was nice. "That doesn't fit with the woman I met in the hallway."

"It does and it doesn't. Her Sunday school teacher and best friend told her she'd be a fool to try it, and I swear she hadn't even ended the call before she was putting on her shoes to come here." He'd been surprised, and a little annoyed, when his mother had called him to pick her up for breakfast and her parasailing tour appointment. But he'd been on autopilot until they arrived at the beach and agreed on a time and a place to meet after her tour. The third time he refused to join her on the boat, she'd stomped off in a huff. His temporary prosthesis would be destroyed in the water. He wasn't even sure he could wear it parasailing. He didn't have his crutch to go without it, and imagining removing it with a crowd watching was terrible.

So here he sat.

An old man holding down a bench or the kid left behind on the school field trip.

Mad at his mother because she hadn't considered all those facts before insisting he bring her here today. That anger had swiftly twisted to depression.

And then Angela had dropped right into the middle of it and he'd forgotten his pain.

"Why aren't you over there with her?" Angela pointed with her chin. "So much fun. Not cool enough for you?"

How much of his angry list should he share? He didn't want to explain his prosthesis, the amputation, the accident that had led to it or any of the worries that came with it. Not yet.

"Not my kind of adventure." There. Good answer. Cool enough without giving away much. "I would be happy holed up at Concord Court, working on my homework, except my mother is also certain that that is a sign of depression. I can't have her dwelling on that. And to be honest, I'd much rather watch her adventures from this bench."

As he said it, Jason realized it was true. Adventure was good for his mother, for everyone.

Was he ever going to have that thrill again?

"Parasail tours in the bay don't measure up to the army, I guess." Angela didn't turn back to him, but he was bracing himself for the questions. Where had he been deployed? What had he done?

The unspoken one would be about injuries

or friends he'd lost in Afghanistan or any-where she might have remembered from a blip on the news. And it would remain un-spoken because those wounds were truths few people wanted to tackle. Only once had a man been brave enough to cross over that line, the surface, to ask about actual combat.

If Jason displayed his prosthesis, that number would increase. He was sure of it. And the last thing he wanted to talk about was combat.

Jason studied his jeans and running shoes and wondered what Angela would say if she knew about his injury and what his life after the adventure was like. Safe. Boring. Lots of staring at white walls and holding down benches.

The screen on her phone lit up again.

"What's with all the messages?" Jason asked, ready to move away from the hard-est stories he had to tell. "Are you an 'influ-encer' or something?" He made air quotes. He hadn't realized he knew how to make air quotes, but there his hands were, all up in the air.

"Hardly. I imagine that's my daughter. I posted a photo I knew would get her attention." Her grin was infectious. She was proud of herself. As she picked up her phone again, a group of cyclists swept past them on the path, stirring up a breeze that blew strands of Angela's hair across his arm.

"That's one thing I missed in my 'welcome to Miami' packet, a warning about the roving bands of men and women on bicycles. They're everywhere." Jason turned to watch them ride away. That was something he could do. Easily. Even with a prosthesis.

"And they're fast." Angela swiped through her photos.

"Gazelles on the Serengeti fast." Jason smiled at her, proud of himself. Parts of him were gone forever. The ability to make conversation with a beautiful woman was still there.

She frowned. "Do gazelles have flashing red tails? I have a hard time picturing red dots disappearing in the tall grass." She pointed at the seats of the last cyclists who were moving around the bend in the boardwalk. In the shade, it was easier to see the safety lights on their seats. "I guess safety matters even in the wild?"

Jason shrugged and returned his arm to

the back of the bench, grateful to roll some of the tension off his shoulders. Puns. Quips. He was rusty, but he could work that out. "I've never actually been to Africa or seen a gazelle in motion. I'll have to do some research on their factory-installed safety features."

The pause before she laughed lasted forever, but the payoff was sweet. So sweet. She giggled. Years disappeared in a poof and he was a dumb kid showing off to impress a pretty girl. War was a world away. Pain and uncertainty and a long stretch of what-do-I-do-now wasn't even on his radar. Just him and a woman and that bubble of emotion he'd mentioned from Smokey's "My Girl."

He wasn't sure if Angela had forgotten his arm on the back of the bench or if she was ignoring it, but she leaned closer to him to show him her phone. "Here's my post."

Jason took her phone and stared hard at the selfie of Angela and some guy dressed like the captain of a ship. "Love boat," Jason read slowly before he turned to face her. They were close. In a different relationship, this could have been a kiss in a second.

Angela seemed proud of herself. Her

hands were clasped together in glee. "Yeah, I couldn't come up with anything better, but I knew it would work to draw Greer in. These other people? Happy bonus."

Moving his arm would be good. He didn't spend time charming women who were with other men. It was sleazy and he'd hope if he ever managed to have his own girlfriend again that other guys would toe the same line.

But he didn't want to move away from her. This place next to her, with the sun and the water. He was truly happy here.

"I felt a bit weird asking for the photo, but it was worth the chance." Angela turned to him. "He had the smoothest move. I asked for a selfie, because captain of the ship"— she made the "so you understand" motion, rolling her hands in the air—"and he put his number in my phone." Her jaw dropped wide open. "What? Who does something like that? Bold is what it is."

"So you just met him?" Jason asked and made a mental note.

"On the boat tour. I saw the summer homes of famous people, took a selfie with the captain and got this cool story. I was so proud of myself, but I don't think I'll call him…" She trailed off, shaking her head. "Why can't I decide? What would I even say?"

"I usually start with 'hello' and go from there." Jason studied her. Did she not understand that any smart man would say yes to her in a heartbeat? "Better decide if you're ready to date a tour-boat captain."

He'd said that with more stink than he should have. The guy was working, earning a living and loving his life. While Jason was limping along. Literally.

"I don't know him." Angela crossed her arms over her chest.

"That's sort of what dating is." Jason fiddled with her phone and pulled up the camera. "How about we take our own selfie?"

Angela leaned away from him while she studied his face. "You're a student. Of mine."

Jason nodded and then held the phone out. "Sure, but I need the practice. I definitely do not selfie enough."

He held off until she leaned closer. When she moved her sunglasses back up to rest on her head, he took the photo. "What should you caption this one?"

She narrowed her eyes as she thought. "It took me forever to come up with the first one. I'll have to think."

A gust tangled her long brown hair over her lips and he was tempted to smooth it away for her. So tempted. He sat there so long imagining a smooth move that Angela took care of it herself. "Aren't you going to put your number into the phone? That's how the rest of this particular maneuver works."

He wanted to.

"Nah, it's pushy." Jason gave her the phone back.

"Okay! I thought so, but…" Angela winced. "I haven't dated since the divorce and I was married forever. Rodney asked me out after a language lab, and I took over from there. I refuse to do that again, to find another guy to organize into a life. I have no idea how anyone gets to know each other today. Who wants to go out with a stranger?"

Organize into a life. The words made him picture her drawing up to-do lists while her husband and daughter fell in line. He'd hate that. Her tone suggested she'd hated it, too.

As a man who had zero plans for what to do after he met his mother, not for the afternoon, the next week, or the next four or five decades in his life, Jason realized he might not be as ready for Angela as he wished. Another reason to crush the crush.

"It's not that different. You call the captain, you talk. That's how dating works. Strangers get to know each other. That is the real adventure," Jason said slowly.

Angela clearly wasn't convinced. Her skepticism was easy to read.

Relieved that the captain wasn't as far ahead as he'd first assumed, Jason stretched. "Text him and ask him to send you a poem. That will tell you all about him. It won't be as good as mine, which you will judge the best poem you've ever read, but it could be adequate."

"I've read Maya Angelou and Walt Whitman and Billy Collins and Langston Hughes. Should I go on? It's not that it won't be good, but the best?" She patted his thigh and then snatched her hand back. "Walk before you run."

Angela cleared her throat and stood with a jerk. "Before class starts Monday." She'd hurried back to the fork she'd paused at when he'd noticed her that afternoon. No ice cream. No water. Just a worried frown to go with her beautiful summer picture.

"Hey, Angela."

She didn't answer, but she did slow and stop to wait for whatever came next.

"When you're ready for me to call you, don't forget to give me your phone, so I can enter my number. And if you want to send me that picture of us, I'd love to have it, but no creeping."

She turned to stare over her shoulder. The desire to hit him with something fun or flirty was on her face, along with a bit of extra pink, but she faced forward and walked away without satisfying either of them.

Still, the day had turned out to be a whole lot more fun than he'd expected.

The twist in his chest was familiar. It had been a long time since he'd hated watching a woman walk away, but that was where he was.

On his bench, like an old-timer, but fighting a junior high school crush.

CHAPTER SEVEN

VERY FEW STUDENTS took advantage of her posted office hours even during the spring or fall semesters, but Angela kept them faithfully. Sawgrass administration expected that, and she wanted to be available to anyone who needed help. The faculty in her department muttered every time she reiterated her expectations about office hours, but today she was the only faculty on hand. Everything was quiet.

That made it easier to appreciate the poems she'd received from Jason Ward. Not only the first assignment, but an extra poem. He'd gone from behind to ahead since their conversation on the bench.

Neither of the poems had titles.

Angela was sympathetic to the struggle. It was often easier to pour her emotions out in a carefully constructed poem, one that might take weeks to perfect, than it was to find the title that fit it. She made a mental note to expand on the importance of titles in class. Meanwhile, here, in her office, she could stare at the words he'd arranged on a page and be impressed.

The first one she'd opened, creatively titled "Assignment Number One," was, on the surface, about ice cream. A universal image that everyone could connect to.

Jason had taken that everyday object and turned it into a consideration of wanting what you can't have. Even more, he took that concept and turned it further to show how hard it was to want something that everyone else could have, would have and maybe not even appreciate, and fear you'd never have it.

Ice cream.

The ice cream she'd held in her hand while they talked on a bench in the shady bend of a popular tourist attraction.

Something so common and recognizable turned on its head to represent distance and yearning.

It was good.

But "Assignment Number Two" was better. The subject? The color red. It was a collection of images and a repetitive rhythm of syllables to suggest a heartbeat or a drum that took a jumble of impressions and created a wild progression of sweet to scary to funny to heartbreaking. This was it.

The loud jangle of her phone interrupted her fourth reading of the poem, and Angela jumped. A quick look at the doorway confirmed she had no audience. That was a relief. She'd forgotten time and place as she read.

"Hello?" she answered as she wiped her eyes.

"Good morning, Dr. Simmons. How is sunny Florida today?" her ex-husband asked.

Since they'd established a pattern, Angela answered, "Sunny, Dr. Simmons." She moved to put the phone on speaker so she didn't get a neck cramp from holding it against her shoulder. They didn't talk often, so this might take a minute.

He chortled like it was the first time they'd ever done that routine. Since it had taken several tense conversations to get to this point of basic friendliness, Angela was willing to play along.

"Good morning, Greer." Angela knew her daughter was in the car. Rodney only called her when Greer was nearby to observe the conversation, and she could make out faint sounds of…road construction? They had to be on the way to work and internship. "You guys are running late this morning."

"Yeah, on top of the never-ending road construction, there are three accidents, which means we live here now, right here on the interstate. Please have our mail forwarded." Greer's dry delivery was sweetly familiar. Resignation was there, as if she almost believed what she was saying.

Her ex continued. "I decided it was an excellent chance to give you a call to talk about all the changes happening in Nashville. I know Greer's kept you updated on the baby and the engagement."

Sure. Along with about twenty posts every day on each social media site. No way would she admit that she was following along at home. "Sure. Congratulations. Have you set the date for the wedding yet?"

There. Nonchalant, but still interested, the same way a truly compassionate emergency room nurse might be when you went in with a sprained ankle. It wasn't life or death, but she would still care. A little.

"We're planning for the first weekend of August. I know it's got to be the worst time to come to Florida, but ever since Greer suggested Key West, we've sort of run with it. I can't believe I've never visited. Ernest Hemingway's home! You remember I did my dissertation on the role of alcohol in numbing trauma in Hemingway's works."

Of course, she did. She'd had to hear about it for months while he was working on it and every now and then when Rodney could get it into conversation. That was more often than she'd expected.

"I sort of recall that," Angela answered and tried to keep the sarcasm out of her tone. If Greer had been beside her, they would have traded eye rolls.

"What was yours again?" Rodney asked.

This was a pretty normal segue. "The role of tradition in Millay's view of modern woman." Her mother had loved to read poetry to her when Angela was a girl. At first, the sounds and the rhyme schemes were what she understood, but it was the language, the poet's voice that had caught her. That dissertation had been a chance to dive deep into a woman's life, a contemporary of Rodney's hero, the man's man, Hemingway. When Hemingway and Millay wrote, the whole world was changing. War was their past and their future, and Millay had embraced every new bit of freedom she gained as a woman in the midst of it all. She'd pushed boundaries. It was a good dissertation, but Rodney wanted to reduce it to a nonserious study of rhyming sonnets.

He'd learned not to express his opinions regarding Millay directly, but his superior intellect was never to be forgotten.

Angela rested her head against the chair. She didn't have to fight this fight anymore.

"Did you guys call just to chat or…" It was time to get the conversation moving.

"Dad's excited to finally make it to Key West. That's where he's going with this." Greer's answer was her attempt at keeping the peace. She'd done that ever since she was a little girl. She never could stand to let them fight.

It was a good reminder that they had no real reason to argue about anything anymore. That was the upside of divorce.

"It will be a beautiful destination for a wedding." That was an easy truth to tell.

Thank goodness something about this could be easy.

"I wasn't sure we were going to manage it, since most of the venues are booked out so far in advance. If we'd tried to wait until the Christmas break, we would have been stuck for sure, but Kate's working with an event planner who has some connection to a guy with a boat. I don't ask many questions. I'll show up with my tuxedo and have faith it will all be perfect."

Since that had been his method of operation for his first wedding, Angela was certain he had no idea how annoying he sounded. He embraced the tradition of the helpless groom faced with a bride's bossiness. Worse, it seemed to please him.

"I hope Kate's not working too hard. Pregnancy can be exhausting and the extra pressure might make that worse. Planning a wedding requires a lot of legwork, even with an event planner to help." There. She'd told him he was edging into jerk territory and reminded him to care for the mother of his child. That had to be her good deed for the day.

Proud of herself, she opened her eyes and

saw Jason Ward standing in her doorway. How long had he been there? He was balanced awkwardly, as if he was measuring the distance for retreat, so she waved him in. Office hours. This was technically his time, not hers.

"I'm in office hours right now and getting ready for my creative writing class." She pointed silently at the chair across her desk when Jason retreated a step.

"Oh, right, your little summer class. How's that going? Have you found this generation's next poet laureate?" Rodney asked. It wasn't so much the words but the tone that prompted her grimace.

Meeting Jason's stare, she rolled her eyes and felt immediately better. She tried to do it only once every time she talked to Rodney.

"My little classes are energizing, Rodney. It's amazing what you get from the most unexpected sources. This morning I read a poem about ice cream that I enjoyed." Angela raised her eyebrows at Jason and he slumped back in his chair. "Not a lot of people get to help something along from good to great, you know? I realize you love your job as the head of the department at a big school, but for me, this class is why I do what I do." There. That felt good, too.

Jason returned the look, his eyebrows raised. She was getting more of the "yeah, right" vibe from his expression.

"Not many kids at little Sawgrass, but you know there's space in my department here. You want to teach your creative writing course, that'll be fine. Take over a couple freshman composition classes. Easy. You say the word, and I'll get you added to my roster," Rodney offered and then paused.

She knew what the word was. *Please*. If she'd only ask him to hire her like it was a favor, he'd do it. Magnanimously. The benevolent man offering his gift to the needy. No. Thank. You.

"This fall semester, you'll have to take the freshman comp classes, but we'll get you out of that eventually."

Right. When she was no longer the new guy in the department, she'd be able to teach what she wanted. Whenever that might happen.

"I'm happy where I am." It was the easiest answer because it was true. "And when

Greer comes down to stay, this place will be paradise."

It would be. Everything she loved would be in one spot.

"Well, that's what I was calling about. Keep the first Saturday in August open, if you don't mind. We haven't sent out the invitations yet, but we'll get them out by the end of the week. Kate and I would love it if you could attend our wedding in Key West. I know it's an extra cost and an imposition that close to the beginning of the new school year, but I am hoping—"

"I'll be there. I wouldn't miss it. I'm hoping you'll find something nautical for Greer to wear, since you'll be on a boat. A sailor suit with one of those little white hats." Angela would show them she was looking forward to the occasion if it killed her. And Greer might for making that suggestion.

"Mom." Greer's long, drawled reply amused Angela, and some of the tense knot in her stomach eased.

"Okay, so you're going to miss out on the chance to wear a parrot on your shoulder and a patch on your eye, too?" Angela asked, her voice shaking with laughter.

"Yes." Greer snorted. Rodney was silent. He never had enjoyed their comedy routines.

"We'll be planning a full weekend, all the adventures Key West has to offer, so bring your swimsuit and lots of sunscreen. Snorkeling tours. A sunset cruise. It'll be fun." Rodney held for a beat. "I saw your post with the captain. Maybe he'd like to come along? You never were good at jumping in with both feet until you had a sidekick. We'll be sure to include a plus-one for every event." Rodney's words were simple enough on the surface, but to Angela, they pressed hard on a sensitive spot. As if his life was fully on track and had left the station, his own sidekick already aboard, while she was still stuck at the gate. Alone.

"He spends enough time on boats, Rodney. This is going to be a celebration for family after all. I'd hate to drag a new... friend into that. Not that he is one. I mean, he isn't anything. Yet. What I mean is, there's no need to add another person for me. I'm happy to come, but I'll be alone." Angela turned her chair to check the view out the window because she didn't want to see Jason's face at this turn in the conversation. Their family banter was okay, but for some reason, she didn't want him to hear anything where she might come off as less than victorious. In the love game, she was losing to her ex-husband and it hadn't even bothered her until this point.

Plus, today she was fumbling and stepping all over her well-thought-out responses. Time to retreat.

"Oh, well, it's kinda lonely to be on your own in a crowd like this, but you know every spot we leave open costs us, so if your plans change closer to the date, let me know. Right now, we'll count you as a single." Rodney sighed. "Finally. The wrecker cleared the lane and traffic is moving. We'll make it home again someday, Greer."

"Hey, Mom, I'll call you later, okay? The senator is going to give me a tour of the Capitol today and I know I'll have some juicy info to share." Her daughter would protect her to the end, but more than anything, she'd twist herself into knots to prevent her parents from fighting.

"Sure thing, baby. I can't wait to hear about it. Call me when you have a minute." Angela's finger hovered over the button to end the call. "And, Rodney, congratulations. Take care of your fiancée, okay?" Before he could answer, Angela disconnected the call and then sagged back in her chair.

For the longest minute she stared up at the ceiling. She was going to have to find out why Jason had stopped in.

Would it happen before their class started?

"So, your ex-husband seems nice." Jason's low voice was a pleasant rumble in the deeply quiet atmosphere of her office. His words surprised a chuckle from her. Embarrassment was so dumb. At some point she'd have to figure out why Rodney's change in circumstances suddenly made her ashamed of everything she'd done for herself.

Later.

"He is nice. In a world of people, some of them really, truly horrible, he's a nice person but…" She turned to meet his stare. "Not without his challenging behavior."

"Challenging behavior. Why does that sound like a therapy phrase?" Jason nodded slowly. "Doesn't think much of your work, I guess. What's his problem? Is he jealous of your success?"

Her success? In a strict comparison of paychecks, Rodney would win, but it was nice to know someone else might view the situation differently. Since "challenging behavior" was Angela repeating what the marriage counselor had said on one of the visits that Rodney had flaked on, Angela was doubly impressed.

Angela fiddled with her phone as she considered that. "He's who he is."

"I haven't read your dissertation, but the description had me hooked." Jason held up a hand. "I'm no college professor, but how many poems has he had published?"

None. The answer to that was zero.

"Thanks. That's a conversation we have pretty often. I don't let it bother me anymore." Half-true anyway. She didn't want to let it bother her.

The last thing she wanted to talk about with one of her students was her ex-husband.

Make that student handsome and add in this…whatever it was between them, and it was time to change the subject. "So, what a nice email to find in my in-box this morning. Not just one poem but two."

Jason's stare moved to focus on the window behind her head. "And then you were… disappointed, maybe? By the quality of the writing."

Angela braced her elbows on the desk and waited for him to look at her.

It took longer than she expected, so either there was something fascinating taking place over her left shoulder or he was really worried about his writing.

"The thing about writing is that the good writers never quite grasp how good they are." Angela shrugged. "Or that's how it goes in my experience. Bad writers have all the confidence in the world, and the good ones… Well, is it bravery? I'm not sure. They keep going even when they aren't sure that what they're doing matters or if it has any value."

"Yeah. That's not just writers. People in general are the same. Bad ones? They'll knock you down and tell you they're doing you a favor." Jason cleared his throat. "I didn't come for a pep talk. I'm here to make sure I can still come to class and expect a solid grade. Is a B still an option? I hoped turning in more than the minimum would help me, even though I missed the deadline."

He hadn't come for a pep talk. Right.

"I would have extended any student the extra time I gave to you. I needed the work before class today. I have it. You've met the requirements. In fact, you've now completed two of the four assignments, so good job." Angela was watching him closely enough that she saw his shoulders relax a fraction. Whatever he thought about creative writing, he wanted the grade.

That was a good start.

He also had talent. She might be the first person to know that, so it was her job to grow it.

"You know what you wrote is good, right?" Angela reached into the drawer at her side and pulled out a copy of the school's literary magazine. "In the fall and spring semesters, we put together a literary magazine. All the work is done by students. Writing, editing, photography, drawing, graphic design. Completely by the student body. You should submit these to the editor. Well, come up with real titles and then submit them."

She slid the magazine across the table. "Keep this copy. I have more."

Jason took it and flipped through a few pages. "Mira. I know her."

When he said it, something clicked for Angela. "Oh, the army. You're retired military. Like Mira. That makes so much sense." If she'd taken a minute to evaluate the whole picture of Jason Ward, it would have been an easy equation. His demeanor. Coming into Sawgrass at his age and without a plan. It was all clear.

"Sense?" Jason asked, a frown sliding into place. This was the Jason she'd seen the first day they met, not like at the marina. He rubbed his knee. "What does that mean?"

Realizing that she was treading right on the line of insulting him, even though she wasn't sure how, Angela said, "You are perfectly pressed in a strictly wash-and-wear environment. I appreciate it. And now that I've read both poems and understand your background, I know how good a writer you are."

Jason tipped his head forward. "Are you distracting me from my question?"

"Not really. You're out of step here. Reserved. Your writing has a lot of passion. This one about the color red? The polish and the flashing safety lights on the bicycles, I got. I wasn't as clear on the connection on the stripes on the flag and blood on fresh bandages, the warning light on the dashboard and the radio tower signal. All red, sure, but some of them don't spring to mind as easily."

She shrugged, hoping that he was taking this as literary criticism, but each word she said crushed her heart. What a life he'd had while she'd been raising her daughter in the safety of middle America. When they'd talked on the bench, he'd mentioned joining the army so casually, briefly, that she'd skipped right over it. How was that possible? It was a huge piece of his life.

"The small pleasures of home made possible by sacrifices people make for their country. It's powerful, Jason." She tapped the literary magazine. "Mira has a poem in this copy. It's about family trees. The images and the themes are different, but you're going to recognize the voice, the truth that she's writing about, how some people make sacrifices that connect them to others they've never met. What we know about people colors how we read their words."

Jason frowned down at the literary magazine. He opened his mouth but changed his mind about whatever he was going to say.

"You know we don't know your experience, the military life, unless someone tells us about it. Mira did. You did." Angela waited until his eyes met hers. "It's hard, but it's amazing. Is Mira retired army, too?" Mira had been fully silent for the first week of class. Angela had been afraid she'd drop it until she read the first poem Mira wrote. All she'd needed was confidence.

Mira had been a solid performer. She'd taken all the lectures and studied how to craft images.

She hadn't had the talent Jason did, but whatever science classroom Mira led in the future was going to get a teacher who experienced things deeply, even if she didn't speak them aloud. And the experiences she'd had… Angela had only seen the smallest tip of the iceberg.

How much more would Jason show?

"No, air force. It's safer to ask which branch." He cleared his throat. "Lots of pride in every branch, you know? Some people would take that army suggestion as a reason to fight."

Angela mimed making a note. "Thank you. I've marked it down for future reference."

"Mira and I are neighbors at Concord Court. She strikes me as someone I'd be happy to fight alongside." He watched Angela closely as he said it. "I imagine you've had other students from there. It's a condition of living there—get a job or get a degree."

Angela tried to remember other military students but couldn't. "Going forward, I hope I'll have others take my classes. Mira's bound for the science building. She wrote a short story about frog dissection that is funnier than you'd expect." She didn't want to speculate about Jason's future. "Do you plan to sign up for more English classes?" He would do well in whatever he chose. The air of unflappable competency that surrounded him convinced her he could do anything he wanted.

What would he enjoy doing, though? Not accounting.

He pinched a pleat in his jeans but didn't

meet her stare. "Not sure what I'll do. I'm still not convinced school is for me. It's weird to have no concept of what comes next."

Angela couldn't imagine living that way. Even when things were falling apart, she'd known what had to be crossed off the list. It was a good thing he was a student. Without that impediment, his hints would have turned into a date, which might have become more.

She'd already proven that taking charge of a man's life didn't work in relationships. Since Jason was all potential at this point and no plan, she would not be able to resist.

However, he was a student. For now.

"Your grade is on track, Jason." Angela pointed at the clock. "Although we both better get to class quickly. And if you were about to ask to take back what you've written, because at least one of my students in every class has attempted to before the critiques begin, you can't. You're committed now." She grinned at his surprise. It never failed. There was always someone who sent her something and then changed their mind. When it was clearly a case of the nerves, her answer was always no. Nerves were part of the process.

"Destination wedding, huh?" His quick change of subject confused her for a second. Rodney and his superiority were already forgotten. That was one of the blessings of moving away and building a new life. Rodney no longer had the ability to ruin her day. "I've been meaning to visit Key West but it's a long drive."

Depending on traffic, about four hours down and back. It was a commitment for anyone unless they had all the time in the world.

"When the semester is over, I'll get down to visit." He stood and crossed his arms over his chest, his attention locked on her.

Was her hair weird? Angela battled the urge to smooth it down.

"I'll definitely be going after the semester is over." Angela mirrored his stance, that unfamiliar but exciting little zing of something prodding her to move, to do something with the energy and nerves bubbling. "And I'll either need to find someone to push me into every activity as the sorry single lady or resign myself to ignoring my ex's poor-you sad face." Angela held up both of her hands. "Not that I'm bitter or anything."

Jason rocked back and bumped the wall. "Never met your husband, but in his spot, I'd be too busy staring at my bride to worry too much about the ex. Date or no date, doesn't change the fact that you've got a whole lot to celebrate yourself. Right? Career. House. Great daughter." Jason tilted his head back. "Have you called the captain?"

"No way!" Angela squawked before she could control it. "Besides, it's only been two days."

And she didn't appreciate the insinuation that she needed a man to find the fun Greer seemed to be demanding, whether he was a date or not. Still, it was easier to do some things with a friend.

"That's more than enough time." Jason's chuckle was enough to turn up the heat under the bubbling. It was harder to breathe and, if she wasn't mistaken, color was filling her cheeks. What was that about?

"In the same place—" Jason shrugged "—I would have called already." He picked up his backpack. "I would definitely need to know when I was seeing you again." Then he pointed at the clock. "About five minutes, right, prof? Better get to class."

He turned away and bumped the doorway on his way out. That slight awkwardness to his exit was the only consolation she had as she thumped back down in her office chair and covered her face with both hands.

Heat.

Excitement.

Breathlessness.

What was her deal?

Angela sat there for a minute to compose herself.

Jason would have called her already.

She wasn't sure what would happen if she phoned the captain of the love boat, whether he'd answer or not.

Angela knew that if Jason Ward ever called her, she'd answer.

And whatever he asked her, the answer would be yes.

CHAPTER EIGHT

WALKING OUT OF the classroom after his first
bout of public criticism felt a bit like how
Jason remembered the last day of school before summer break. He'd been through a lot
and now there was nothing but freedom on
the other side.

At least Angela had been there for it all.

Getting her verdict before class started
had been what he needed to make it through.
When he'd stopped in at her office before
class, he'd been on the verge of telling her
he'd drop out of the class, Sawgrass University and public life if she'd give him the two
poems back.

No one should experience the sweaty
panic he'd suffered when he imagined people reading his words.

He'd done hard things.

Forcing himself to come to class that
morning had required real fortitude.

Then she'd said it was good.

And he'd realized it didn't matter so much what other people thought. Angela approved. She was the expert. The Poet expected him to write more and better.

The feedback from his "peers," the eleven people suffering a summer semester class with him, had barely registered. Their notes about the titles were expected. He needed to work on those.

Looking up to find Angela staring at him…

Expected wasn't the right word but he hadn't been shocked, either.

He'd caught her attention as he'd left her office before class. That last line of his had been good. As good a line as he'd ever delivered. And it was true.

Without the class and the student-teacher thing and the whole problem with his amputation, he'd have called her more than once already. Not as many times as he'd pulled his phone out to consider light social media stalking that week, but enough that she'd have no doubt he was into her.

That ship captain was a fool for not asking her out on the spot.

Shaking his head as he walked, Jason dug around in his pocket for his keys. A woman from his class, Nikki, was propped against the wall outside the door. "Hey." He hadn't made many friends at Sawgrass. He hadn't tried. The age difference was a lot.

"Hey," she called before trotting down the steps, "your stuff was good."

Jason stopped. That was nice. "Thanks." He shifted the backpack he'd decided to get to fit in. "Have we read anything of yours yet?" He was sure he'd remember. Everything she'd said in class was smart.

"I turned in a poem but we haven't read it yet. I don't know if I can make myself turn anything else in. The nerves are killing me. I better drop the class." Nikki bit her lip. The conflict was clear on her face.

And Jason knew where she was coming from.

"I get that." He glanced back at the building, hoping that Angela was headed in their direction. He could let Angela give her a pep talk. No luck. "I had the same problem. Sent my stuff in late, but Dr. Simmons was nice enough to grant the extension. She also gave me feedback on my work before class, so I had some armor going in. She'd do the same for you."

Nikki stared hard at her flip-flops while Jason waited. Were they done? He didn't feel like he could walk off yet.

"At least give it a shot. You thought you wanted to be a writer or you wouldn't have signed up for the class." She hadn't said a word about the easy A on the first day. "It's okay to be afraid. This gives you a chance to show how brave you are." He'd had a drill sergeant say that once, right before he'd bellowed how worthless the whole unit was. Someone had gotten a letter from home that included a pillow with the phrase stitched on it. It worked better here.

Eventually, she nodded. "Good advice. Thanks."

He returned her nod and watched her run back up the steps. He'd done his good deed for the day.

When he stepped carefully off the curb into the parking lot, relaxing as his leg held, he noticed a tiny blue convertible blocking his truck. His mother.

"How was school?" she asked, one arm draped over the door as she watched him approach. "You're moving almost like you trust that leg again."

Jason slowed to a stop. "What are you doing here?"

His mother whipped off her sunglasses. "Is that any way to speak to your mother?"

Jason tipped his head back and studied the bright blue sky. In his opinion, his tone had been fine. Since they had no plans together that would require blocking his truck, his question was reasonable.

"Sorry, Mom." He cleared his throat. "What are you doing here?"

She huffed out a breath. What other way was there to ask the question?

"I made you an appointment with the prosthetist we met in the hospital. If we go now, instead of fighting about why you don't need to go or how it's too soon or how a new leg for running is too expensive or why you don't need me holding your hand, we might even make it on time." She tapped her fingers in a rapid rhythm on the door.

"An ambush. Is that what this is?" Jason asked. He'd wanted to enjoy his day a bit longer.

"Yep. Get in." She pointed at the passenger seat. "Daylight's wasting. I have a sunset cruise around the harbor planned and I don't want to miss it."

Since it was early afternoon, Jason wondered how long this appointment was going to last. "Fine. We can argue on the way, but let me drive." He wanted to be in control. His mother might rearrange his life, but at least he could be behind the wheel. "Park and hop in my truck."

"I can't leave my car here. I don't have a parking sticker." She grinned widely. "Besides that, I don't trust you."

Jason dropped his backpack in the gap between the front seat and the trunk. Two seats. She was lucky he had a truck. "You don't trust me. I've done everything you suggested. Concord Court. Sawgrass University."

"Creative writing instead of accounting. A complete and total lack of any life outside of Concord Court and Sawgrass University. I wouldn't say *everything*." His mother sniffed. "Buckle your seat belt."

Jason followed orders and braced one arm on the door. If he had any friends here, he might be concerned about how being driven in this tiny car by his mother would damage his manly reputation. Finally, a bright side to being a social outcast.

She patted his hand. "Once we do this, get you back out and running, and we consider a new prosthesis for daily wear, one that matches your activity, your life will change again. You won't be a dull hermit anymore." The parking lot was almost empty, so she accelerated quickly and turned out toward the main road as Angela Simmons paused on the curb. "Oh, good. I was hoping your friend might show up. She's pretty. You should ask her out, get her to show you around. Might have to ask her twice. Bet she's got options."

Since he had watched Angela's eyes spark when he'd told her he would have already made the call, Jason was certain he knew what her answer would be when he got the opportunity to ask.

Had he told his mother she was his professor? No.

He might regret that. It would have made this moment a bit less awkward. Or more. With his mother it was hard to say whether that would have deterred her from braking in front of Angela or compelled her to stop.

Besides that, he'd already tried the tour guide as dinner companion angle.

"Hello there! I'm so happy we've had a chance to run into you again." Mae Ward's public voice was sugary sweet, as if she'd never met a stranger. "How is your summer going?"

Jason blinked up at Angela, curious about how she'd take the situation. She straightened the strap on her shoulder, checked with him for something—he wasn't sure what—and said, "My summer is going well. I have a great class. Students with so much talent."

Then she tilted her head to the side, as if she was assessing what his mother said to that.

Jason turned to see what his mother thought about this. Now she knew Angela was a professor.

"Oh, isn't that nice." His mother tightened her hands on the steering wheel. "And what do you teach?"

Jason tipped his head down. The quiet had been nice while it lasted.

"Creative writing. Your son is a good

writer." Angela was trying an innocent expression, but the amusement gleamed in the shadows of her eyes. She was enjoying this.

His mother tilted her head to the side as she studied him. "Well, now, that does not surprise me a bit." But it did. He hadn't told her about the Poet because he knew she'd never stop encouraging him to ask her out.

He'd had a couple weeks of breathing room.

"Are you off to some new adventure today? I've always wanted to try parasailing. How was it?" Angela asked as she crossed her arms over her chest. He had his suspicion that she was lying about the desire to try parasailing, but she'd said it twice now. At some point, he'd have to believe her and that would be a problem. "I ran into Jason while you were both at the marina this weekend."

Jason closed his eyes. Now he was really going to hear about it.

It must have taken a minute for his mother to recover.

"I will tell you I enjoyed it more than I thought I would. I mostly went because someone told me I couldn't. I confess that's a surefire way to make me prove I can." His mother tapped his hand. "Works on all of us Wards, doesn't it?"

There was no good way to answer that, so Jason stared straight ahead.

"You got any people in your life that know exactly how to push your buttons? Some people need to be dared. Others need to be shoved real hard out of the nest. One or two won't budge until you're dragging 'em like one of them weightlifters that pull trains with their teeth or some such." His mother waved her hand airily. "The worst ones? They take all three. Jason's one of those. I couldn't get him out parasailing, but I haven't given up."

He scratched his chin and wondered how far his mother would go.

"A pretty lady might get farther faster than his old mother has." She took off her sunglasses. "You ask him to go parasailing sometime. Let's test my theory."

Before Angela could shut that down, Jason said, "She's my professor, Mom. Dr. Simmons operates with professionalism and high standards. You wouldn't want to strain those, would you?"

His mother's jaw dropped.

"Well, not for two more weeks anyway." Angela widened her eyes as he looked at her. Was his mouth hanging open? "Adventure can wait that long. I can see the resemblance between the two of you."

His mother's smothered chuckle was cute, but it was nothing compared to the devilish pleasure Angela was taking in the moment.

"Two weeks, huh?" his mother drawled. "I'm a hold you to that, hon. You have a real good afternoon." She put the car in Drive and pulled away from the curb, her obvious pleasure growing with every rotation of the tires. "I like her."

Jason did, too, but some of his confidence drained away. "How do I measure up against the options when I have to tell her I can't go parasailing. Or worse, when I have to toddle off like an old man while she's out there soaring. I wish you hadn't done that."

His mother stopped abruptly at the stoplight. "Now, you listen here. You cannot live the rest of your life afraid to do the things you want to do. There's no way I'm going to let that happen. If I have to rope in every pretty girl that crosses your path, hijack you to deliver you to whatever professional I can find to help, or fill your ear nonstop, I will do so. You are my son. I love you. I almost lost you and I will not allow you to throw away a perfectly good life because it's going to be different than you expected. Do you hear me?"

Jason shifted in his seat. That tone brought back memories. She'd asked, "Do you hear me?" in that tone at the end of every single dress-down she'd delivered. Over eighteen years, he'd learned it very well.

"I do hear you, but what makes you think you can work miracles?" Jason asked. "There are limits for everyone. I had 'em before, too. It's just… They're a whole lot closer." He straightened his legs and wished for one quick second for a pair of shorts. "Will jeans work for this visit?" The stray question popped out of his mouth before he realized it. He didn't want to go and it had nothing to do with his clothes.

A cheerful beep from behind them convinced his mother to accelerate again. How long the light had been green neither one of them could guess. As she navigated the streets and the interstates toward the veterans' hospital, Jason rested his head against the seat and enjoyed the hot breeze in his hair. A convertible had seemed like a foolish choice for his mother. She'd need more seats, more room, better safety features. But that afternoon, the wind in his hair was medicine.

The parking deck attached to the hospital was cooler, and there was very little moving when they made it in, but his mother snagged one of the compact car spaces and turned off the engine. "Grab that bag behind my seat. They wanted to do an evaluation, so I brought you a change of clothes and shoes."

Of course she had. Jason was shaking his head when he yanked out the bag. "Mom, you're going to have to learn I need to do things on my own schedule."

She slid her sunglasses onto her head. "Fine. Tell me why your schedule has changed."

Confused, Jason dropped the bag into his lap. "What do you mean?"

"You've never had an ounce of patience in your life. At eighteen, you could not stand the idea of wasting four years at a college, so you enlisted. What did you say? You wanted to live." She tapped his cheek. "Where did that go? Your surgery was over months ago. Were you planning to die on my couch, son? Physical therapy. That was the only reason you left the house, and I guess that was because you didn't want Terry coming to get you. She's little but she's scary. Concord Court. Sawgrass. Even this creative writing class. You wouldn't have done any of it, and how does it make you feel now?"

Jason studied the concrete pillar in front of the car. "You're right, but you don't know what it's like to consider life with this prosthesis. Parasailing? How would I even manage that? I'll be lucky to afford one prosthetic leg and it won't be for water or swimming, so it's crutches. Removing my leg while everyone stares and pities me. Giving up parasailing saves me all that, so what's the harm in not doing it?"

The anger was back.

She sighed. "Not wanting to go parasailing? Okay. I guess I get that. Even being afraid of parasailing itself. The height. The water. Whatever. Those things I get. Being afraid to try it because you have to remove your prosthesis? I don't get that." She grabbed his hand and squeezed hard. "You are a hero. That's what I see. That's what other people will see. And if they don't? Who cares?" The last words were almost a shout. "You have one life to live. Forget those people and do what you want. It's you and me here. Forget Rosette and your daddy and whatever you thought it was to be a man before your accident. Some of that—maybe most of it, I don't know—is gone, but you're going to live a good life if I have to drag you kicking and screaming. You see if I don't. Now get out of this car. We've got an appointment and it's rude to keep people waiting." She swung around, opened her door and slid out while Jason was processing.

The anger. Jason stared at his balled-up fist. Then he realized how ridiculous the situation was, a loud argument in a deserted parking deck.

"It's rude to keep people waiting but shouting at them in a parking space is perfectly acceptable behavior." He slid out and walked around to meet her. "Aren't you going to put the roof up?"

She blinked slowly at him. "It's a rental.

I bought the crazy insurance. It'll be fine."
Then she straightened her hat and shook out
her skirt. "I wasn't shouting. I was being
emphatic."

He was laughing as she marched away to
punch the elevator button that would take
them to the ground. "Emphatic is loud sometimes."

"Yes, it is." She stared hard at the numbers over the elevator, her shoulders hunched
tightly.

"You sure I'm ready to talk to the doctor? What if I need to heal more? Build my
strength?" Jason draped his arm over her
shoulder and waited for her to relax against
him. His mother was a force of nature, one
who'd convinced countless kids to fall in
line through the years. She hadn't lost a bit
of that iron will in retirement.

"I talked with several different people before I set this up. You're ready for the evaluation physically. I don't know if you ever
will be mentally." The elevator doors opened
and she stepped inside.

Failure was a hard thing to face. If he
had to guess, that was what his mother was
afraid of. Failing him.

"Okay, so we'll do the evaluation." Jason stepped back out on the sidewalk across from the entrance when the elevator doors opened. "'I'll never be ready mentally.' I don't like the way that sounds."

She snorted. "Right. That's the part that got to you, a potential threat to your manliness."

It stung when she put it that way. "I meant more about wasting one's life, but whatever."

"Uh-huh." She wasn't buying it.

They navigated the hospital and found the waiting room for the prosthetist before she continued the conversation. "You're a poet now. Interesting."

His inward groan was long and loud but Jason maintained a firm grip on his voice when he said, "Thanks for not outing my trip here."

His mother shook her head. "That girl has brains. Smart is written all over her. If she can get over the rest of your issues, why would your missing foot chase her away?"

Issues? When she said that, his problems seemed more like quirks than real challenges. Before he could argue that it was so much more than all that, the nurse called his name and he was caught up in the evaluation. His gait was observed while he walked and ran, his measurements were taken, and he was forced to sit still while a large machine made precise three-dimensional images.

"Okay, we've got what we need to work up the permanent prosthesis, but I wanted to talk to you about the questions you answered the first time we talked, before you left the hospital." The best prosthetist in town was dressed like the students in Jason's creative writing class. His T-shirt and scrubs were clean enough, but neither had met an iron. There was no mistaking his expertise, though. Every question Jason's mother asked was answered thoroughly and confidently. "It says here you only want to be able to walk, run maybe. Guy like you, with your background in the military and your fitness level, I'd expect you to want more than that. Now, we don't have to do everything all at once. This is an expensive process for most people, so if you decide you want to expand your options, we can work on a specialized prosthesis then, but it worries me, these answers. You don't ask the questions of a man who is determined to get his life back together." He tapped his clipboard and studied Jason's face. "Anything changed since we talked?"

One quick glance at his mother showed a woman who was strenuously biting her tongue. She wanted desperately to have every one of Jason's medical team on her side in the tug-of-war.

"I guess…" Jason took a deep breath and forced himself to exhale slowly. "I've always been a runner, but I just… With this…" He pointed at where his leg stopped. "I don't know my limits anymore."

"None. Anything you want to attempt. Somewhere, people do it every day." The prosthetist crossed his arms. "For running, we'll do some gait training and you'll be set. A specialized running prosthesis can improve your speed, your endurance, your agility. You could be a better runner than you were before." He stared over his glasses. "But you aren't sure because…"

"I don't like the attention I get when my prosthesis shows or when I'm on crutches and everything that I'm missing is on display. Pity. A million invasive questions

I don't want to answer. It's a lot." Jason brushed a hand over the skin on his knee and pretended to study a scar. He'd said it out loud to someone other than his mother. Was this a breakthrough?

"Therapy. That's what you need. Along with a permanent prosthesis with all the cosmetic bells and whistles, and another for running that makes you appear half human, half cyborg." He set his clipboard down. "You can have it all now. You gotta grab it. Group therapy, individual—I don't know, but you need to give it a shot. And when your prosthesis is adjusted and fitted properly, you'll join one of our running groups. A whole bunch of men and women in great physical shape, running on prostheses. Everything is easier in a group, right?"

Jason considered that while he ignored the way his mother was silently nodding in agreement. It was good advice.

"Thanks. I'll find a group." The memory of the midnight gathering around the pool went through his mind. They might function as a support group, but only if he told the whole truth. "Concord Court has lots of support information available, so I know where to start."

"Your physician is a good place, too, but it's nice to have Concord Court here. Everything *is* easier in a group, and you've got a whole bunch of people there who understand what you're going through better than the rest of us ever will." He offered his hand to shake. "We'll get to work and give you a call when it's time for your final fitting. For now, though, swimming is great exercise. No prosthesis needed."

"I've been thinking about trying it." Jason picked up the sleeve to put his prosthesis back on. "What about biking? Might be the most popular hobby in southern Florida."

His prosthetist removed his glasses. "Also good exercise. The bike will require modification, clips to ensure your prosthesis stays on the pedal, but there's not too much else required. If it's something you're passionate about, really love, we can work on a prosthesis that allows more free movement. Let's get you running and we can talk about what comes next. Swimming's the same. Do it now if you want, no prosthesis needed, and then when you're ready, with the right equipment, it's hard to find an activity that isn't improved. Life could be, too."

"Swimming for now. We'll see how the new leg works for running." If he could get his head wrapped around the fact that the change in his body was a bigger thing to him, in his head, than it would be to anyone else, he might have already done it.

His mother was quiet. So very quiet.

Until he'd changed his clothes again and they were back in the car.

"Gonna take up swimming, are you?" She pointed her finger. "You will enjoy that."

And she'd hold him to it. Jason didn't say anything until she pulled up back in front of his truck at Sawgrass. She didn't, either. If he didn't say something, both of them were going to end up sleeping in the car because she was going to wait until he spoke or die trying.

"Thanks, Mom." He smiled slightly. "I needed that kick in the pants and I didn't know it."

She wrapped her arms around his shoulders and squeezed hard. "That's what I'm here for, and I brought my kicking shoes." She sniffed. "And you know if I don't see progress on this therapy front, that will be the next battle we'll wage. Don't make me do that, son." She patted his cheek and then leaned back, the sparkle in her eyes clear.

"I'll drop in and talk to Reyna tomorrow. All services scheduled through Concord Court go through her office." Jason stretched the muscles in his arms. His mother had been tossing that in since he'd opened his eyes in the hospital. Terry had mentioned therapy groups while she'd put him through the paces in physical therapy. Now the prosthetist had added his two cents. The consensus was overwhelming.

No matter how certain he was that he could and should adjust to his changed life alone, he was going to give in. Not gracefully, but he'd give therapy a shot.

"Talk to her today. Now, get out of my car. I've got to change clothes before my cruise." His mother had both hands on the steering wheel.

"Is this a booze cruise?" Jason asked as he got out of the car. "Why didn't you ask me to go with you?" He'd have said no, but he would have had fewer good excuses to get out of it than the parasailing tour.

"It's a singles' cruise, and I did not want you cramping my style." She lifted one hand in a wave and then sped through the parking lot. She was still grinning when she turned back onto the main road.

When he pulled into the spot in front of his townhome, Mira Peters was jogging past. "Join me. One more lap and then I'm headed to the pool to cool off."

Jason didn't even pause. "How about I meet you at the pool?"

She shrugged. "See you there." And then she was gone.

He dumped his bag inside the bathroom and went to dig up his old trunks. Was he going to do this?

If he put it off, life would get in the way and the next time he considered it, the decision would be twice as hard. As he removed his prosthesis and the umbrella, the cool air on his skin was nice. Ignoring the voice in his head that promised him a nap would be even better than a swim and less trouble, Jason grabbed his crutch, took a towel from the clean laundry on his sofa and headed for the pool.

He'd beaten Mira. Now he had to find the

perfect place to stash his crutch, and then he'd get in the water. He was still studying his choices when she opened the gate. One split-second pause was the only reaction Mira gave when she noticed his amputation. "Need help with that?"

She held out a hand to take his crutch. His pride in his throat, Jason offered it to her. Before he could figure out what to say in response to her help, she had a hand on the middle of his chest. With one quick push, the how of getting into the water was gone. He was in the blessedly cool water and she was laughing at him from the side. "I'll put this down in the shade. Let me know when you want it." When she leaned it next to the gate, Jason realized he could reach it himself if he had to. He would lift himself up on the side of the pool to sit and turn to reach the crutch. Easy as that. She was better at this than he was.

"Thanks for the encouragement." Jason wiped the water off his face. "I needed it."

She didn't answer. Instead, she yelled, "Cannonball!" and hit the water hard, the splash washing over Jason again. When she came up grinning, he returned the favor with a huge wave of water.

"Hey, no horseplay in the pool. Reyna will see you." Sean Wakefield was coming into the pool from the direction of the office. "And then she'll send me out here to warn you that Concord Court is not responsible for pool injuries." He pretended to consider. "Since I've already done that, go ahead."

"Are you off duty? Join us." Mira waved at the empty pool. "Plenty of space, even for your ego. I could race you and beat you."

He faked a laugh and, not for the first time, Jason wondered if there was something between them.

"I prefer my pool dark and quiet. I'll catch you guys tonight." Sean raised his eyebrows at Jason. "This means you. I want to know why we didn't hear more about your exciting experiences with the army doctors." He paused with one hand on the gate and pointed at the crutch. "You know you gotta talk that stuff through, man."

Jason tipped his chin up. "Turning over a new leaf. I'll tell you all about it tonight."

Sean narrowed his eyes. "Don't make management angry, please. I have a secu-

rity camera malfunction to straighten out."
Then he was gone.

"What's his story?" Jason asked.

Mira shook her head. "Everybody's got
one. He better tell you his."

Jason enjoyed treading water for a minute.
"Someone told me you were a poet. Is that
part of your story? You didn't share that part."

Mira shrugged.

"Good enough to be published." Jason
dipped his head in the water, enjoying every
second. It was nice to have a friend to give
grief over something as easy as her poetry.
This was what he'd miss if he let his pride
bring him down. Friends. People who knew
his story and still shoved him in the pool. No
walking on eggshells or careful handling.

"I'm better at science." Mira kicked over
to the side of the pool. "I enjoyed the class,
though."

"Angela's pretty great." Jason experi-
mented with his legs, loving how easy it
was to move through the water.

"Angela? Guess Reyna is a distant memory. Dating the teacher is a tricky maneuver,
soldier." Mira saluted. "Brave."

"Not dating. Not yet." Jason moved down

to the end of the pool. "But that's my new leaf. The brave one."

"Sean's right about this, at least. You gotta talk. If you don't, what we've been through will tear you down." Mira joined him. "I like Angela a lot. You seem all right. I give my blessing." She motioned with a stiff arm to each of his shoulders.

"What is that?" Jason asked.

"You're a knight. I'm a queen. My arm is a sword." She rolled her eyes. "You're supposed to be creative."

Jason raised his eyebrows and whistled silently. "More than that, I'm competitive. Want to race? Three laps? Loser brings the beer tonight?"

Mira pursed her lips. "Fine. I'm out of beer anyway." Then she pushed off from the wall into a fast breaststroke. Jason grinned as he followed her.

CHAPTER NINE

WHEN THE NEXT Saturday rolled around, Greer called and interrupted Angela's investigation on social media, and it was a good thing, too. With June weddings and family vacations and then all of the great news coming from her ex-husband, she'd built a pretty dark cloud over her head.

"Happy Saturday, baby," Angela said as she stood up to change rooms. Staring at her laptop was not going to make anything better. Her intention had been to write, but she was too easily sidetracked. "What have you got planned for the day?"

"Today, we are painting the nursery. Dad has some important meeting at the office, so Kate and I are going to be able to work without his supervision." Greer's emphasis on "supervision" was a big clue as to how she viewed her father's management style. She wasn't a fan, either.

"That will be fun. Kate's lucky to have your help. When you were on the way, I kept picking up one thing here and one thing there. By the time we managed to move into a bigger apartment and set up a nursery, I was afraid I had so much stuff there wasn't room for a baby anymore." They had been so young and too dumb to be afraid of the change that was coming. That had to be the best way to welcome a baby.

"Yeah, get ready for a whole lot of before and after shots. Kate watches home improvement channels the same way you watch cooking shows." Greer cleared her throat. "And yet, neither one of you puts all that study to work. Weird."

Angela shook her head as she studied her empty refrigerator. Obviously she'd found her Saturday purpose. What fun. Grocery shopping. "Listen, if I ever need to find a use for dragon fruit and matcha tea, I'll be ready. Kate's been prepping for this nursery. You'll see. All that study will come in handy." She closed the refrigerator door.

"Maybe." A quiet Greer always rattled Angela. Her daughter was about accomplishing tasks. She didn't waste time, so if she was on the phone but not speaking, something big was coming.

"I hope your dad's helping with this. Kate has a lot on her plate." The itch to fill out Kate's to-do list was strong. She was spending too much time with Kate electronically.

"A little. Kate's not like you. If he's not involved, she waits until he's ready. We are all spending so much time together." Greer's dry delivery was hard to read.

Angela relaxed against the sink. "Tell me. Whatever it is. It will be fine, Greer." They'd always been able to talk. Angela hoped the physical distance between them wouldn't change that.

"I'm worried about you, Mom." Greer coughed. Was she crying? "For so long, we were all kind of frozen in place. Dad and I were here, and nothing changed much after the divorce. Even Kate didn't shake things up, but now…"

Angela waited patiently for Greer to finish, even as every word twisted the knot in her stomach tighter.

"We're moving on. Are we leaving you behind? Am I?" The last words were said in a rush, so it took a minute for Angela to decipher them. Then the hurt hit and she had to breathe through it. That low-level anxiety that she had been afraid to study for too long because she didn't want to put a name to it had tumbled from her daughter's mouth, a direct hit.

Conscious that it was up to her to fix this, Angela turned to look out the window over her sink. "Listen…" What was she going to say here? "You and I, we're connected. No matter how far or fast you go, that connection sticks. Trust that. I do. I trust that. I know you better than anyone and I love you and even if you fly away, I know that you'll come home. This stuff with your dad? It has nothing to do with me." It didn't, even if she was entirely too invested in developments in Nashville. The only tie she had was through Greer.

"I shouldn't enjoy all this as much as I do, Mom. That's all. It's fun to shop for a baby. I never knew. Kate and I almost got thrown out of the home improvement store last night because they were closing and we were still pulling paint chips. Kate bought paint last week, but it's still so much fun to dream up all the possibilities and we have so much fun together. It might have been the level of noise we were making. Kate would read a paint color name and strike a funny pose. I giggled every time." Greer exhaled slowly. "Why do I feel guilty saying that?"

Angela crossed an arm tightly over her chest to dull the ache that sprang to life at Greer's confession. "That's no way to live, baby. And honestly, if you knew about all the things I'm doing…" She was about to make up huge lies, the biggest she'd ever told her daughter, but there was no way this could continue.

"Is it the boat guy?" Greer immediately asked, her tone scandalized. "Are you having a romantic adventure?"

Because that was the only solution Greer would understand. Angela groaned loudly. Her daughter, the romantic. How easy it would be to murmur something noncommittal to get out of the conversation. If the boat guy was hanging around, Greer would feel better, which would relieve Angela, and life would go on.

Until the inevitable minute where she was expected to produce the boat guy as her plus-one on a yacht out of Key West and then…

Short of a solid breakup story, she'd be stuck.

Even with a believable story about how boat guy had turned out to be terrible or boring or both, Greer would be disappointed and this worry would pop back up.

"Baby, a man is not the answer." Imaginary or otherwise. Whatever might be stalled in her own life, Angela firmly believed it and she needed Greer to understand it. "I don't blame you for hoping boat guy or someone else can fix everything. I did for a long time, too. The world sort of tells us that. I made decisions based on that fear for a long time, but we don't have to live that way. Look at what I've managed. I'm proud of my life and I'm happy with it."

Greer's grumbling was expected, but Angela laughed anyway.

"No one is saying that, Mother. You have an awesome job, a great place, all of that. It's not about an 'answer.' It's about are you having any fun? That's it. Boat guy could be fun. Climbing Everest could be fun. Singing karaoke could be fun. What are you doing that is fun? I'm having a blast this summer. My internship is a blast. I love sitting in meetings and taking notes and typing them up and making copies. I love it. This baby stuff? Fun. Dress shopping for a Key West wedding? You should see some of the things Kate had me try on. I'm doing it, but sometimes I worry that you're sitting in your office, grimly maintaining office hours that no one else cares about, just because there's a rule. Do you understand what I am saying? Forget the feminist girl power. I've got a handle on that. Do you understand what I'm asking?"

Angela took a calming breath. "I certainly don't have any problem hearing you because you are shouting in my ear, Greer Elizabeth Simmons."

Greer didn't groan this time, but there was a distinct edge in her tone when she said, "Sorry."

Silence pulsed on the call while Angela tried to craft an answer to Greer's passionate speech. Her dismissal of Angela's concern as "feminist girl power" stuff was irritating, even if Angela was glad her daughter knew her own strength.

Fun. What sixteen-year-old kid wondered if their mother was having any fun?

"Sure, I have fun." She wouldn't mention loving her job. Greer knew that already.

Angela flipped through the junk mail on the counter and racked her brain to find an answer. She'd done too good a job at teaching Greer to take care of others. It had come back to bite her.

Her visit to the marina had worked to dispel some of Greer's worry and to give her own spirits a boost. What other activity could she toss out to appease Greer? Parasailing immediately popped up, but there was no way she was doing that alone.

The longer she stood there, the harder it was to think of anything other than parasailing. In every image in her mind, she wasn't alone. Jason Ward was her partner in adventure.

The postcard at the bottom of the pile caught her eye. A Cuban food festival in Little Havana. Surely she was brave enough to park her car, find something to eat and take some photos. Would it be enough?

Worth a shot. "What I'm getting from this conversation is that I need to share more with you and with the world via social media about how I'm spending my time. That must be the measuring stick. I've been craving a Cuban sandwich. Remember that place we visited when you were here? The one that was voted number one in Miami?"

"Yeah. It was in a strip mall or something and you did not want to go in," Greer answered.

But she hadn't backed down. Her daughter and her daughter's opinion had always mattered more than her own fears. "So the atmosphere wasn't what I expected. That sandwich? So very good." If she'd read the menu before she and Greer had stopped in, Angela might have hesitated to order the special—she was known in Nashville as a picky eater. But she hadn't, and when her sandwich had arrived, piled high with roast pork and good things, Angela had taken one look at Greer's dubious face and dived in.

Angela hadn't forgotten that sandwich since, and the longer she thought about it, the better her idea seemed.

"I'll be sure to post photos far and wide, baby. You stop worrying. Enjoy every minute of this summer. It is filled with good things that you will want to remember. Worrying about me? That's going to rob you of the joy, so don't do it. We are both exactly where we need to be right now." Angela sighed. "And the next time you go dress shopping with Kate, text me photos. I have no idea what to wear to a yacht wedding, and I don't want to show up in my bathing suit if everyone else is in formal wear."

Greer's laughter was sweet. Such a relief. "You in a bathing suit? Never gonna happen, and definitely not when there's a photographer around. I hoped you might change your mind about water when you moved to the beach, but…" Her silence shouted "just saying" clearly.

"It's the sand that bothers me, not the water." Although, to be fair, deep, dark water was another issue. Bathtubs she was okay with.

"You get to painting. Send me pictures. I'll be sure to post photos of the food festival." Angela waited patiently until Greer agreed and vanished from the call. She was worried. She was also a teenage girl with a limited attention span.

Angela pushed her phone across the

counter and studied the postcard. "At least it isn't parasailing."

Without worrying about all the obstacles, although parking and not knowing much about Little Havana came to mind, Angela slipped on her sandals and grabbed her keys. She was committed. Greer would be expecting photos.

The drive was quick, and before she was prepared, Angela had squeezed her car into a parking spot three streets over from what appeared to be the epicenter of the festival, Domino Park. People spilled off the sidewalks here and there, and music filled the air. If she'd wanted a party, she'd found it. To be safe, Angela sprayed a cloud of sunscreen over herself, paid the parking meter and assessed her options. Food trucks lined the street she was on and the smells were delicious.

Since it was still early, she decided to move closer to the park. The day she and Greer had passed by, it was a shady oasis. Small groups were clustered around tables, but it had been peaceful. Today, it was filled with people of all shapes, sizes and ages. There was a small stage off to one side. Angela managed to catch a toddler who was heading for a run-on collision with her knee and waved off the mother's grateful thanks. Greer had always been the same. Once she had a goal in mind, she put her head down and moved, no matter all the tripping obstacles in the way.

The reminder of her daughter was a good reason to pull out her phone. She took a picture of the crowd and pondered what to post for entirely too long. That could be the problem. If she'd post the photo instead of giving up when she couldn't come up with clever words, the pictures could speak for themselves. Once she'd satisfied her own photo requirement, Angela moved closer to one of the groups to watch a game of dominoes in progress. Intent on the action and trying to understand the rules, Angela moved too close to the person standing next to her. As she turned to apologize, she realized she was standing next to Jason Ward's mother. Since the woman was paying no attention to her, Angela craned her neck left and right to find Jason.

"He's parking. Dropped me off so he didn't have to listen to my directions. I don't

know if he'll ever find a spot for that big ol'
truck. I told him my convertible was a better
choice, but he doubted my parking ability."
She scoffed. How had she guessed Angela
was hunting for Jason?

"Angela, isn't it? Is it all right if I call
you that? 'Doctor' seems so fussy between
friends. And you better call me Mae. Don't
try anything else, you hear?" She tapped
her straw hat down as if that was that and
everything was settled.

"I can't decide if Miami is the smallest
big town in the world or..." Angela wasn't
going to say it.

"Ha, it's almost as if the universe wants
you and Jason to run into each other." His
mother's eyes were wide and innocent. Angela had a feeling if anyone wanted them to
run into each other, it wasn't the universe.
"You do not know how long I had to talk
to that boy to get him out here. Used every
trick I had and finally he decided he could
stand to have one of those Cuban pastries
I brought him. I came down last weekend.
Less crowded, and I had the best little bites
of guava and cream cheese treats. The boy
fairly lit up at the suggestion." She shook her

head. "What is it they say about the way to a man's stomach?"

"It's his heart, Mama, not his stomach. Nobody wants to claim a man's stomach, trust me." Jason stood behind them, one corner of his mouth turned up. "Are you two in this together somehow?"

Mae slapped a hand across her chest. "I am scandalized you would suggest such a thing. This is pure coincidence, a meeting of adventurous people who refuse to meld to the couch on Saturday. This is what you would have missed if I'd let you get away with it. Angela and I are adventurous women who know what is up." She waved a hand toward Angela like she was displaying top prize on a game show. "You are welcome."

Before Jason could say anything to that, one of the older gentlemen at the table asked if anyone wanted to learn to play, and Mae whipped around, threw her hand in the air and jumped up and down for good measure. When he pointed at her and motioned her forward, she yelled, "Meet you back here in an hour. Do not stand around." She didn't turn to verify that Jason accepted her orders.

Instead, Mae plunged through the noisy crowd and slipped into a spot at the table.

Angela watched Jason decide whether he was going to do as he'd been told. He shifted back and forth on his feet. Even in the mid-day heat, he'd gone with crisp jeans and a button-down.

"At this point, she won't know if you ignore her orders just to prove you can. She's preoccupied. Why don't we go find food and hunt up a bench?" Angela studied his face while she waited. He was more relaxed than when they'd first met but still entirely too serious for a Saturday.

"Good idea. Those pastries are the only reason I'm here. Restaurant or food truck? Easy or exciting?" Jason asked, a half step closer to the food trucks than the last time she'd noticed his stance.

"I'm supposed to be coming up with an exciting life for social media. Food trucks." Angela shifted closer to him as a large group of people speaking Spanish swept through the crowd. The little girl she'd caught before they both had big bruises was riding on the shoulders of her father while her mother gestured toward the food trucks.

Jason placed a hand in the middle of Angela's back and everything in the world became sharper, clearer.

"I don't want to lose you," he said close to her ear. "Not in this crowd." Then he followed in the wake of the family ahead of them, his hand an anchor connecting the two of them. When they made it to the long line of trucks, he said, "This could take a while." The crowd milled in and out.

"What if we split up?" Angela asked, determined not to put anything extra on his touch. At some point, the crowd would clear out and he'd step back and everything would be normal. "I'll grab two Cubanos, and you choose the pastries."

She craned her neck to see over the crowd. Away from the domino tables and the pedestrian area, along the edge of the tiny park with a view of nothing special, were benches scattered in the shade of a huge banyan tree. "And we'll meet at the benches over there." She needed to focus on her sandwich. That was why she wanted to find another bench, not because it would be an opportunity to talk with Jason again. Of course. There couldn't be anything between them because he was a student. One who wrote things she enjoyed reading, but that was all. For now.

"Good plan." The slide of his hand across her back stopped her breath, and when he stepped away, everything dimmed.

"Not great, Angela," she muttered to herself. She refused to think about what all that might mean as she stood in the longest line for a sandwich. She trusted other people to lead her to the best sandwich. While she waited, she tried to come up with safe topics to cover. His writing, which they'd covered pretty well already, and...

The person in front of her stepped away and it was time to order. "What's the best sandwich you have? I need two of them."

The young woman tipped her head sideways and then shook it. She turned to yell, *"Dos Calle Ochos, por favor."* Then she held out her hand. "That'll be fifteen dollars."

Angela did not argue. She handed over her card, took it back and moved swiftly to the side when the woman pointed toward the second window. Where she would wait. Obviously.

By the time her order landed in the window, Angela was sorry she hadn't also ordered a couple of drinks. Fingers crossed that Jason would think more clearly, she took the wrapped sandwiches. When the second young woman in the truck hollered at her, Angela turned back, and two bottles of water were thrust in her direction. Angela took them gratefully and headed for the park.

Jason had already claimed one of the benches. If she had to guess, she'd say he had also dipped into the bulging bag at his side while he waited—flakes of pastry dotted the sidewalk at his feet. "I was starting to worry you'd made a run for it." He took a water from her and then one of the wrapped sandwiches. "Or got a better offer like you did the last time."

Angela frowned as she positioned her food and drink carefully. "Better offer? What happened last time?"

"The captain." Jason fluttered his eyelashes.

"He's really in your head, isn't he?" Angela asked. "To keep you up to date, there have been no calls or texts exchanged and he also occupies too much space in my daughter's head." It could be a real problem.

"And don't forget your ex. He brought the guy up on the phone call." Jason took a big bite of his sandwich, paused and then closed his eyes. "Oh my. Delicious."

So that captain was occupying space in everyone's brain except hers.

Jason's mention of her ex-husband was irritating. It reminded her that Rodney was taking up valuable real estate in her own mind.

Neither one of them spoke as they ate. The sandwich was as good as the one she'd had at Miami's number one Cuban bakery, but the atmosphere was so much better. From where they sat, she could hear conversation in English and Spanish, guitar and violin music coming from different directions, and birds and a light breeze stirring the branches of the trees in the park. Even the shaded heat and humidity of their bench was right. It all fitted.

"Almost like we've left Florida for someplace new, right?" Jason asked as he balled up the wrapper. "That was delicious. If I have to tell my mother she was right again, at least I'll have eaten well."

"Mothers enjoy it when their kids say

'you were right,' so you'll be making her week." Angela crossed one leg over the other and tapped her foot to the song that existed only in her head. "Never argue with your mother."

He sipped his water. "She's on a roll of being right lately."

Angela chewed the last bite of her perfect sandwich and then washed it down. "And it burns, huh?"

He sighed and draped his arm along the back of the bench, his thumb brushing the bare skin of Angela's arm.

"I might be coming around to the same realization about my daughter." Angela shook her head. "And it burns. At least your mother has the wisdom of age on her side. My daughter…" She couldn't even come up with the words to express it.

"She sounded smart on the phone, and her face is a copy of yours. I expect she'll be right a lot in her life." Jason stretched out his legs.

"She is. It's just…" Angela balled up the paper in her hand. "Did you ever worry that your mother wasn't having enough fun?"

He grunted. "You've met my mother,

right? No doubt she's found her element."
Mae Ward was probably the undefeated
domino queen now.

"I mean when you were a kid. Did you
ever worry your mother should be doing
more for fun? The thought never crossed
my mind." It hadn't. Why would it have?

"Well, no, it never did. I enlisted without
a single worry about what it would do to
my mother. No guilt then, but boy, I'm deal-
ing with it now. Greer's ahead of schedule.
Could be good for both of you. Less therapy
in the future."

"Right now, it's too much pressure for
me," Angela said and held a hand to her
chest. "I'm starting to wonder if I should
hire an adventure coach. You heard that
phone call. No one has high expectations
for my ability to keep up with all the events
at this wedding."

"But you want to prove them all wrong."
Jason sipped his water. "Or at least the ex-
husband."

Angela turned her head slowly. "You don't
have any exes hanging around that know
how to push all the wrong buttons?" Be-

cause his comment had sounded a bit judgmental.

He pointed at her. "Valid point. I've never been married. I've only been close once. When it came down to leaving home, she couldn't do it and I couldn't stay. What do I know about buttons?"

"Hmm. Falling in love is easy. Keeping it takes work." The music drifted between them, and his acknowledgment was enough to soothe her irritation.

"We've already got to go parasailing to make your mother happy. Want to be my adventure coach? My guide?" Angela asked before she thought better of it. "I'm guessing skydiving, bungee jumping, rock climbing... Those are nothing to a soldier." And he'd have to physically catch her and strap her into the harness to get her rock climbing, but she wasn't going to mention that.

"Why does 'guide' make me think of uniforms and learning to make fires to earn badges? People talk about skydiving as if it's hard." Jason shook his head. "It's one step. Then you just fall. Falling is easy."

"But you've got to stick the landing...or else," Angela drawled. His chuckle sent that fizzy spark through her. She was the funniest woman in the world at that moment.

"Yeah. There's a metaphor there." He straightened his leg and his face tightened.

"Okay, is that a yes to skydiving, then?" Angela asked, even though she was nearly certain there was no way either of them were going to jump out of a plane for fun.

"Wouldn't it be easier to find a date to the wedding?" Jason asked.

"In the short term? Yes, it would be easier. I know the perfect guy." Angela paused when she realized what she'd said. When Greer had first demanded she do that, Angela couldn't have named one possible option. Now there was no question who she'd ask. She could do it right this second.

"But this whole 'worrying about Mom' problem needs a better solution, I guess." Jason waved a hand. "You made it here without any coaching. You're doing fine. No coach needed."

A soft no to her proposition, then. He wouldn't be joining her for adventures. Fine. Some of the sparkle of the afternoon dimmed.

Jason offered her his bag of pastries with one hand. "Try this."

Dissatisfied with his answer, Angela took one of the pastries, the ooze of filling landing on her thumb before she managed to get it to her mouth. To avoid a mess, she put the bite-size pastry in her mouth and then licked off the filling. An explosion of tart guava caught her off guard.

As she chewed, she closed her eyes because the whole experience was sweet. This place. This perfect bite. And when she opened her eyes, her companion on the bench was watching her closely.

"Delicious." Angela pointed at the bag. "Dangerous."

He nodded. "I was thinking exactly the same thing." His tone. His eyes locked to hers.

As little as she knew about flirting with men who weren't Rodney Simmons, Angela was certain Jason wanted to kiss her. Right there, in that perfect moment, did a kiss make any sense? It was the only way to make something so perfect any better.

Before she could scoot closer to him, one thought flitted through her brain.

He's a student. For two more weeks, you have no business kissing him.

Ignoring her ethics or the voice of her

conscience or whatever it was that kept her from making bad, but exciting decisions, would have been easy.

The loud blare of horns and drums from the stage was her first speed bump.

The second bump brought her to a stop.

"You kids are missing everything over here," Mae Ward said from her spot behind the bench. "The whole world's having a party and you're gathered by the appetizers." She motioned at their empty sacks. "You *ate* all the appetizers, more like."

They had to wait to answer while the emcee of the afternoon's concert rolled off the names of the acts who would be appearing on the small stage.

"Time to get up." His mother made a herding motion with her hands. "There's dancing going on, children."

Ready to give it a shot, if only to spend more time in this daydream, Angela turned to Jason.

The scowl was back.

CHAPTER TEN

HAD IT BEEN an hour already? Jason stared over his shoulder at his mother, biting back the question. It hadn't been. She'd spotted them and made up her mind that they needed to make a change.

And, in the process, had robbed him of the perfect chance to kiss Angela.

No one could have blamed them.

Could he get the moment back?

"We're fine here. Thank you." He would have tried to make a subtle "beat it" motion with his head, but she would have asked what was wrong with his neck.

As he watched his mother brace her hands on her hips, a sinking sensation settled in his gut. She wasn't going to drop this. She'd decided something should be done for his "own good." When she got that notion, nothing changed it.

One small hope remained. Angela might want to stay right here with him.

That would save him the awkward duty of wiggling out of dancing.

Since he was barely managing walking on the prosthesis—the occasional swelling that still struck when he tried to do too much combined with the day's heat had given him fits just that morning—he was certain dancing would be a bad adventure.

Humiliation was to be avoided at all cost.

Before he could frame the question in a way that would convince her that she didn't really want to go out there and move around in the heat with half of Miami, Angela said, "Salsa. They're teaching beginners. It could be fun." Her eyes were bright. Excited.

Her answer hung in the air while he occupied himself with carefully folding his bag of leftover pastries. He could humiliate himself by rudely extracting himself from this spot, or by dancing. Small group versus large group.

While his mother watched with a worried frown and Angela waited, he had to make a decision. He could refuse and walk away, leaving behind the smell of weird and anti-social as he escaped.

Or he could give this a shot.

"Don't lose this bag." He shoved the pastries at his mother and held his hand out to Angela. "One dance. I'm in this for one."

They both beamed at him like he was a hero.

Angela waved her phone at his mother. "Can you take a picture? Only if we're good enough. When I trip over my feet and drag Jason down with me, make sure the camera is off."

"No falling." Jason had to put that out in the universe.

"Since my middle name is not grace, I can't make you any promises." Angela tugged him over to the small group of kids and seniors rocking forward and back while a beautiful woman in a short dress and heels counted to eight and clapped in time.

"Back together. Rest on four and eight," she yelled.

The upside to realizing he'd forgotten how to count to eight on his own was that Angela had her head down, frowning with concentration as she watched each step. All of his stutter steps and landing behind the beat meant nothing to her. She was fighting her own battle.

"Now we try with partners," the dancer leading the how-to yelled. "Find a partner."

Angela's grin was huge and he couldn't help but answer it as she slipped into his arms. They mimicked the stance required and slowly practiced the back-and-forth, the lead and the follow.

"This is fun," she said in his ear. The music and chatter of conversation meant she had to step close. The buzz of her voice tingled down his spine and he broke the hold to pull her closer. They managed to keep on the beat but totally ignored the teacher's demonstration of the next progression. Right here was enough for him, and Angela didn't object.

"Oh, your mother is taking a picture." Angela shook her head. "Greer is never going to believe I did this without one."

The music changed. The horns grew louder, so Jason decided to move them away from the stage. He wanted time with Angela, not hearing loss.

And this was when it always happened.

He got too comfortable, stopped being so careful. He was falling before he knew it and landed on the scrubby grass with an undignified curse.

"That rock. It jumped out and got you." Angela offered him her hand. "I saw it. I can pick it out of a lineup if you want to press charges."

As if she had any hope of getting him off the ground.

He would have smiled, but the music was too loud, the heat was unbearable, and his heart was pounding in his chest.

Before he could work through the slow process he'd taught himself for when he fell, he was surrounded on all sides by men. In half a second, they'd hoisted him to standing, patted his back and brushed off the grass, and returned to their partners.

The disorientation was still with him. The weird heaviness in his muscles that came with the shock of every fall.

Anger that this was his life now and forever welled up. Staying here would double his chance of losing control.

More than anything, he wanted to sit somewhere cool and quiet. He needed space.

His mother was frozen in the background. Angela held her hand out, ready to go back to their elementary salsa dance.

"Actually, the heat is getting to me." He rubbed his stomach. "Too much cream cheese, I guess." He didn't meet Angela's stare. The pinch of settling in on the prosthesis had gotten familiar, but he couldn't point to it and tell himself it was right. That little twinge would go away. "And I have some homework to catch up on. Wouldn't want to fail my class."

He didn't want to see her disappointment, so Jason turned away from Angela and did his best not to limp as he walked toward his mother. "Meet me where I dropped you off, in ten minutes. Can you tell time, Mom?"

She pursed her lips and nodded once, annoyance clear in the high color on her cheeks.

Jason turned back to try some halfway normal goodbye, but Angela followed him. "Are you okay? Did you twist something when you fell?"

"I'll walk it off." Determined to get out of there without more embarrassment, Jason steadily, slowly, carefully walked off.

All the way to his truck, a loud conversation in his head tumbled his "should have" and "why didn't I" thoughts. Back in the truck, with the air-conditioning full blast, Jason took stock. His knee ached. There would be a bruise, smaller than the dent to his ego.

CHAPTER ELEVEN

WHAT HAD HAPPENED? They'd been having a great time.

Or she had.

Angela chewed her lip and considered chasing Jason down to demand an explanation.

But he didn't owe her that.

"Sunny to thundershowers like the weather around here," Mae murmured. "Sorry about that. You young people were doing fine on your bench. I shouldn't have interfered." She offered Angela her phone. "I did get a real cute shot of the two of you, you with a grin to light up the dark, for sure."

Angela slipped her phone in her pocket and studied Mae Ward's face. If she didn't know better, Angela would assume everything was fine. "If you and I synchronized our calendars, it would be less of a sur-

prise the next time we run into each other."
Clever. She was hoping for clever.

Because the fact that her feelings were
hurt by Jason's cold shoulder would be an
awkward conversation to have with the
man's mother.

"Children are a challenge, Angela. The
challenge changes when they're grown, but
it does not disappear." Mae tipped her chin
up. "I taught him manners, but I can't en-
force them the way I used to."

Angela shaded her eyes to check on Jason's
progress, but he'd turned a corner. "I understand. My daughter thinks she's the mother
now. I get how we lose control once they
learn to drive."

Then she noticed Mae's face. She was
worried about her son. Angela was confused
and a little annoyed. A grown man could recover from tripping in public without running away. "Should we go after him?"

Mae snorted. "No. The answer to that is a
certain no. That boy is a carbon copy of his
daddy. Better give him some space to realize
how silly he's being, and so stubborn." The jut
of her chin suggested some of Jason's stubborn nature had come from her.

"It's nice to be able to blame all my daughter's problems on her father. I mean, they do belong squarely on his shoulders, even if I'm the one who moved hours away from her." The lump in her stomach hurt. She didn't understand Jason's anger. Her mouth was dry.

Mae sighed. "Well, now, if we're going to go for true confession time, I might bear a pinch of the blame for the fact that Jason is determined to never be seen as weak. I must have told him a thousand different times when he was growing up that Wards don't cry over spilled milk."

Angela tangled her fingers together as she watched Mae shift back and forth on her feet.

Then she realized that the responsibility for a lot of Greer's concern for her landed squarely on her own shoulders, too. She'd taught her daughter to always have a plan. It made perfect sense she'd build a to-do list to fix Angela.

"But I'll undo some of that if it's the last thing I do." Mae's eyes met Angela's. "You still have time, too."

It was hard to pretend they didn't understand each other after that. They were both mothers. They'd both done the best they could for their kids and still had to face the realization that they'd failed, left some weak spots.

"When he was a boy, he was the one in his group with his head on straight. Some of the wildest kids you ever met came out of Rosette High School and I had a front-row seat to watch all that. But Jason, he could calm down situations or encourage kids who needed it. He was the captain of every team he ever played on, not because he campaigned, but because other people trusted him to lead. All I ever wanted for him was everything. Not the army. Not..." She waved a hand as if she couldn't continue.

"I'm guessing you didn't dream of him becoming an accountant, not really." Angela squeezed her hands tightly together. She was out of her depth. If someone wanted to tell her that Greer couldn't make her dreams come true, Angela would make them regret it. They would fail and regret attempting that conversation forever.

But she'd never imagine she could tell Greer what to dream for her life, either.

"Jason is not meant for accounting," Mae said and took her hat off to use it as a fan. Dark curls were flattened to her head. "I do know he's stubborn. If I tell him one thing, he'll do another." Her shoulders slumped. "And right now, if I'm not pushing, he's going to stop moving altogether." Mae bit her lip and Angela fought the urge to jump into the silence. Whatever it was the woman wanted to say, she wasn't sure she should.

Angela knew this had to be it, the thing that caused Jason's personality to change in a heartbeat when threatened with nothing more than college registration or dancing at a Cuban festival. This was his secret hurt and his mother was dying to say something about it.

But Mae knew it wasn't her place to tell.

"I…" Angela rubbed her forehead as she planned her words. "I don't know what it is that's causing him this setback, but I'm going through life changes myself. It can knock you off your stride easily." Angela waved her phone. "Thus, the posting of pictures on social media when I could not care any less about it." She sniffed. "I could also be lying to myself, because this is such a pride thing for me."

Mae leaned forward quickly. "Go on. Pride?"

Unnerved to have Mae's close attention, Angela fiddled with the edge of her phone. "Yes. It's one thing to be dissatisfied with my life. I don't know if I am. I love my job and I'm doing what I'm meant to do. My poetry has been absent for a bit, but everything else is smooth. No bumps. My daughter and I talk every day, and she's thriving. Everything that she wants is coming to her. Good job. Nice place to live. She's a happy kid. There is nothing else to worry about." She met Mae's stare. "Then my ex-husband announced his engagement to his pregnant girlfriend in a social media post with the Eiffel Tower as backdrop. All of a sudden, I'm just…"

Angela shook her head. She couldn't admit her obsession with daily updates or fears that Greer would be unhappy, or worse, so happy that she'd never want to visit Miami again. Selfish. These worries in her head were so selfish.

Mae patted her shoulder. "That is a lot to

absorb, honey. I don't blame you for losing your footing."

Relieved, Angela said, "You don't? I mean, it's all good." For them. It was all good for them. "And it shouldn't have an effect on me." It shouldn't, but somehow it did? And if she could figure that part out, she could solve her own stupid problem.

"That's bound to have some ripples." Mae nodded. "And this world is determined to tell every woman over… I don't know, sixteen, that a good man could end all her troubles. Your daughter wants you to be in love, am I right?"

Angela closed her eyes. "Yes, and that's the last thing I want to reinforce in my daughter's head."

"Yeah, sons never mention that, and the suggestion you might go on a singles' cruise gives them indigestion." Mae's long sigh provoked a smile. It was the world-weary tone of a woman who'd been down that road too many times. "Try standing in the funeral home and forcing yourself not to murder a Sunday school teacher for listing all the single men your age in the church. At my husband's service. It was a good thing I was so shocked. Otherwise, I'd have a mug shot and a wild story to tell about beating someone with a guest book. Rosette, Georgia, would still be whispering about me in scandalized tones." Her eyes met Angela's. It was a horrifying story but the perfect illustration to her point. Mae's chuckle made it okay to laugh out loud.

"I'm glad you didn't have to do jail time, Mae." Angela wiped the tears under her lashes away. "It's so ridiculous."

Mae agreed. "It is. Doesn't mean they don't have a point, though."

Angela rolled her eyes. "Not you, too!"

"I do still have a son that admires you. A lot. And since he's the most handsome man in these United States and a military hero to boot, it's my duty as your friend to make sure you don't miss your shot." Mae waved her hand nonchalantly. "It's a favor from me to you. Also, I've done life both ways. Lots to be said about finding the man who makes all that good stuff so much better."

Angela rubbed her forehead. The heat was overwhelming. Jason was the only one of them with any sense. "He's great, but his mood changes are…" What? What did they mean? "I wish I understood them."

"Military. Post-traumatic stress disorder. This loss veterans have when they leave the service, like the world drops away and everything they've relied on is gone. You don't have to know Jason at all to understand how that can change a person's mood, right?" Mae said. Her lips were firm. This was a fight that mattered to her.

Angela studied her face. Mae was trying to tell her something important without telling her. "Right. I've seen news stories where people struggle with all those things. When Concord Court opened, there was an article that listed all the programs that would be offered to help veterans. Education. Employment. The owners work with the veterans' hospital to help with care and recovery and even substance abuse. Correct?"

Mae was watching, waiting. Did Jason need help with alcohol or drugs? Was that it? In Angela's mind, that was the only reason he might not tell the world about whatever it was. Even if that was the case, he should have nothing to feel ashamed of if he was getting help.

He'd hate being under the control of an addiction.

"I guess I still don't get it," Angela said, frustrated because there was something that needed to be said and no one would say it. "And this reading between the lines to figure out the truth? I don't want to do that now. I did it for almost twenty years with another guy and I am telling you, even if I'm alone every day until I disintegrate into dust, I don't want to twist myself into knots anymore."

Mae's lips flattened into a line. Had Angela gone too far?

"The best thing about growing older is learning that lesson right there, hon." Mae squeezed her arm. "You know what you want. Sort of. All I'd say is that those things that you and I know about that Jason might have experienced and how he can handle all of it, they're true, but the part I struggle with and you need to examine is this." She leaned forward. There was no mistaking how important whatever it was she was going to say would be, so Angela mirrored her action. "He's going to get all this. He's going to learn to deal with the memories and the wounds, but it takes time." She pointed her finger. "You understand what I'm saying? Happens for all of us. My husband died, and that rage at having men pushed at me is gone. We all gotta work through these things one day at a time. We can't jump from here to there and expect anything to work correctly when we're done."

She patted Angela's hand again. "I've had to remind myself of this more than once. Those mood changes? They aren't mine to fix. He's the only one who can do that, but I do love him. I know he'll do it. He'll jump this hurdle. Even now, he's the best man I know. Tomorrow or next week, he'll be even better."

Mae plopped her hat back on her head. "Your problem is focus. We always want what other people have. You're seeing good changes. If your ex-husband was going through a breakup and losing his job, you'd be content to let him handle those ripples all by himself."

Angela had thought the same thing herself, yet she still had nothing but questions for Mae. However, Jason pulled up beside them on the sidewalk. Mae moved to climb up into the truck.

Angela held out a hand to stop her. "Hey, thanks for this." She waved her phone. "I'll post it and buy myself some time until I can find someone to go parasailing with me." That someone would not be Jason. He was not even acknowledging her standing there on the sidewalk.

"I enjoyed parasailing," Mae said as she wrinkled her nose, "but you're going to have a hard time convincing Jason right now. Remember what I said about time. A year from now? He'll be dragging you by the hand to do whatever off-the-wall, in-the-deep-end-of-the-ocean thing you want to do. I believe that with my whole heart. It's a matter of time. And if anyone could convince him to try it next week or next month, it might be you." She tapped her temple. "Time."

"Thanks for the advice about my own change. I'd decided the best way to handle this envy or jealousy or whatever it is that I'm experiencing—but don't want to label because I'm pretty sure it's selfishness—is to have great adventures. I was sort of hoping he could help me with those but…" She shrugged a shoulder. "I want Greer to understand how full life can be without the man the world says we need."

"All the while relying on a man to get you there." Mae frowned. "I follow what you're saying, but I fell through the hole in your logic."

Angela laughed reluctantly as she realized that Mae was right. How silly.

"Or..." Mae wrapped her arm through Angela's. "Now I'm spitballing, so if I end up in a big ol' logic loophole like you did, forgive me, but you have two ways of looking at this. You want to go parasailing? Call me. I'm in and I already put all my information in your contacts. You could even tell your daughter and ex and friends that you were doing me a service or something."

And no Jason, not unless she counted the surly guy sitting it out on the bench.

"What's your other option?" Angela asked. She was not going to explain that the winning choice would include more Jason. The Jason who offered her sweet pastries and talked easily about nothing. That was what she wanted.

"You could treat every day as an adventure. Take a picture of a great lunch view. Check. Try a new dessert. Check. And do them with the sidekick that makes everything exciting because you are not going to fool me. When I interrupted your taste test, you were on an adventure and about half a second from having the time of your life." Mae shook Angela's arm. "My mistake. I pushed him too hard. Learn from that and don't get in your own way."

Angela frowned as she considered that. "I am out today all on my own. I didn't need any help for that."

Mae winked. "But the adventure didn't start until he was there, am I right?"

Angela blinked and did her best to ignore the weight on her chest.

Mae was right. Angela wouldn't tell her that because even in her own head that set off bells. Warning bells? Maybe. Or the kind that go off when someone hits the bull's-eye at the fair. Mae might wish they were wedding bells.

"I like you, Angela." Mae nodded firmly. "No way I'll stop pushing him. Somebody has to, and I'm his mama so he'll love me no matter what. For you? You meet him where he is.

"Don't you hate old women who hand out free advice you never asked for?" She winked and opened the truck door.

As Angela watched them drive off, she understood what Mae meant.

Dancing had been fun.

Angela had enjoyed flirting with Jason more.

And if they'd managed the kiss hovering between them, this would have been a day she'd never forget.

Whatever was between them, Angela believed today's confusion would remain until Jason could tell her why he didn't want to dance or do any of the things she'd called adventure. But they had to finish this class first. Nothing else mattered until it was over.

CHAPTER TWELVE

HE WAS A man afraid of what other people might think about him.

And his mother was giving him the silent treatment. It didn't happen often. He should be enjoying it more.

Since he might as well have been a five-year-old sulking after a tantrum, he understood the impulse.

The white-hot anger had receded. Disgust with himself and his own mood swings had replaced it.

As he turned down the street to his mother's apartment, Mae drawled, "Do your skills with the ladies seem rusty to you? Because I'd hate to imagine this is how you've operated around the world, son. That might explain why I do not currently have grandchildren to show off. The one thing they don't tell you when you decide to take the leap into an 'active retirement community' is that grandchildren are our number one bragging rights. If you don't have them, you sit quietly until the opening conversation, the one that begins every single meeting and outing, is over." She held up one hand. "I know. That makes no sense. It happens even at my upscale assisted-living facility, where I'm busy with all sorts of activities, doing things I've wanted to try for a long time. Parasailing? That was a big deal to me, and it was completely eclipsed by the birth of twins. We're fully functioning adults with our own lives here, but grandchildren are important. I would like to have some."

She never came at him from the direction he expected.

"I overreacted. All I could focus on was sitting somewhere, taking stock and cooling off. I've done that." Jason tightened his hands on the steering wheel. "And my skills might be rusty, but that can be fixed."

His mother snorted. "Can it? How soon? That girl was confused. Hurt, even." His mother shook her head. "Have you done anything about finding a therapy group?"

When he'd been on active duty and daydreaming about retirement, Jason had listened to all kinds of horror stories about guys who couldn't make it back home. They lost their way and ended up in jail or addicted to something that helped them make it through the hours.

Jason had pitied them, certain he'd never be that weak.

When he was swamped by emotions he had no control over, he knew the edge was closer than he expected.

His mother was holding the line for him. All his life, he'd held himself to a higher standard, believed he had to be stronger, but now he realized failing was a possibility. That edge he'd been certain he'd never see, much less fall into the darkness on the other side…it came closer sometimes. At midnight, when he couldn't sleep and there was no hope of distraction until sunrise. The anger he hated prowled nearby. The edge was right there. When he'd left Angela standing on the sidewalk, the shame had been huge. Without his mother, he'd sit with that shame.

He'd never warned his mother about the anger, but she knew him well enough to understand that she had to stand strong and push him away from the edge.

What a burden to put on one tiny woman.

It was no wonder she had to push twenty-five hours a day, eight days a week. If she lost any ground against the edge, she might never get it back. School. Doctors. Therapy. Even this thing with Angela. Mae was scrambling for handholds.

"Not yet. Not exactly. Therapy…" Jason trailed off as he stopped in front of his mother's unit. "It's for big problems. I can handle this." He wanted to. He would. He should be able to.

He hoped he could manage to get a grip before Angela Simmons got tired of waiting.

"Therapy is exactly for this, Jason." His mother grabbed his arm and waited for him to face her. "It's for exactly this. You were wounded. You could have died. Your life is… Well, everything was wiped clean and you're starting at the beginning. None of that is easy. And I am warning you, that girl is worth doing whatever it takes to avoid another meltdown."

He wanted to argue. Her worry was clear. Every line on her face was proof of the nights she'd done some staring up at her own ceiling. She'd mentioned how she'd feared for his safety while he'd been deployed. Mentioned? She'd harangued him about it to get him enrolled at Sawgrass.

But the fact was she'd been holding the line for him since he'd woken up in the hospital stateside.

"I'm talking with this group of vets, Mom. Believe me when I say I understand I can't swallow all this." Her shoulders relaxed. Telling a half-truth made her relax. "When it comes to this leg and the whole 'wound' thing, I don't want to talk about that."

"You don't want to talk to me. You don't want to tell your friends about it. Find someone you don't care about, pay them some money to listen to you complain or admit whatever it is you're afraid of. You're like everybody else, JJ, no better, no matter what your mama always said." She shook her finger at him. "If you'd been here, you'd know that one of your favorite people needed some help with grief once upon a time." She blinked at him while she waited for him to catch up. His mother had seen a therapist?

She pinched the bridge of her nose as she always did when she needed extra patience. Jason could remember her doing that outside his first Sunday school class when he'd argued that Santa Claus brought the greatest gifts instead of Jesus. Mrs. Peabody had not appreciated his opinion that day.

"When your daddy died, I was lost." She blinked rapidly. Whatever Jason said would be wasted breath. "My only other family in this entire world was in Afghanistan." She swallowed hard. "I'd lost your father and I could lose you at any minute. All I had was the house and the town that was smothering me." His mother inhaled slowly to exhale carefully. "For months, I paid a perfectly pleasant stranger to listen to me talk, and she didn't interrupt me to say what a hero you were or how time heals all wounds or how not a single day is guaranteed here. Friends, strangers, they all wanted to say something comforting and not a one had the good sense to stick with 'I'm sorry.'"

She wagged her head rapidly. "It's like they never lost someone they loved. They wanted the magic words that would get them out of the tough spot of talking to me in my grief. That therapist? She got furious along with me and that let me know it was okay to hate sympathy cards from my insurance agent and the bank. Everything I thought and could not say out loud to another soul? She told me I was fine. Those things were logical. Normal. Expected. All part of the process. I could get mad at your father for not taking better care of himself and at you for leaving and at my mailman who kept bringing the bills from the hospital even though we've been friends since first grade. None of it had to make sense. And that's what it took for me to get through, the understanding that I didn't have to pretend my life was the same but just figure out what it was going to be on the other side."

Jason pulled his mother closer, wrapping his arms around her until her head was on his shoulder. She was crying. He hated that. That much pain deserved to be washed away with tears. He'd come home for his father's funeral, but he'd had orders, so he'd prioritized what had to be done on his trip. Holding his mother like this had not made the list.

"I'm sorry, Mama." He squeezed her tighter. "I'm sorry. You shouldn't have had to do all that by yourself. I should have been there. I'm sorry."

Angela's daughter was worried about her mother having her own life. He'd been too wrapped up in his own world to grieve with his. His mother had deserved better.

Her sigh was both tired and relieved. "I'm getting through your thick skull, but it's a real slow process, honey."

Jason waited for her chuckle as she rested against him.

"I didn't tell you that to get an apology. I wanted you to understand there's all kinds of reasons to talk to someone, big and small, and really, the size is the least important piece. Honestly, I learned the big problems and the small annoyances are all tied together." She tilted her head to the side. "And I decided then I wasn't going to wait to do what I wanted with my life, not anymore. Safety is nice, but it's not as good as real happiness. If you have to make a fool of yourself to be happy, wouldn't you want to give it a shot?"

Jason did rub the ache in his head then.

It was all so much to think about, to do, to try for the first time.

"When do you have to sign up for fall classes?" his mother asked, the small grin on her face proof that she knew she was giving the conversation a swerve.

"End of July. I have time." Which was a good thing. He still didn't know what he wanted to do with the rest of his life. At this point, he wouldn't even cross off dancing. Something about his mother's advice had lit the spark of hope again. She was good at that.

"I'm not sure you have an accountant's personality. An accountant would have done something other than storm off, leaving a pretty girl wondering what had gone wrong." She tapped her lips. "Better ask about jobs in therapy, too."

She was unlocking the door to her unit before he could come up with a response.

Since any reply would have been unimpressive, Jason reversed out of the parking spot and drove to Concord Court. Mira was churning up waves in the pool, but he wanted time before he had to make more conversation, so he parked outside of his townhome, let himself in and almost flopped down on the couch.

The first order of business was changing clothes. Jeans in Miami in June were a bad idea, but he didn't have a better one. At home, he always changed into shorts and removed the prosthesis to let his skin dry out.

Once that was done, he made himself another sandwich, grabbed a beer from the fridge and settled down on the couch. This was all he needed: time to regroup.

But he was no good at sitting still for long. When writing a travel piece for class turned into web searches about finding a therapist and job counseling and personality tests to determine careers and watching videos of people with prostheses dancing and running and whatever he could dream of, Jason tossed the computer aside on the couch and rested his head on a cushion to stare up at the ceiling.

All the evidence pointed to one overwhelming answer.

There was only one thing keeping him from doing all the things he could dream up: his own mind.

Before he could overthink it, before he could put on his full armor, Jason put on his prosthesis, grabbed his keys and headed for the Concord Court office.

Reyna was behind the desk when he

walked in. She glanced up when he opened the door and was watching him when he dropped into the seat opposite her desk.

No expression.

It was clear she'd been a ranking military officer. Alert waiting. That was her constant setting.

"Did we have an appointment?" she asked before propping her elbow on the desk.

"No. I'd offer to make one and come back but this is something I need to talk about now." He cleared his throat. "You mentioned a therapist working with vets. Could I get a referral?"

She pulled open a drawer. "It's all in your paperwork, Ward. No need for any approval." She slid a business card across the table and he picked up a whiff of exasperation. "I might give that up. None of you spend a second reading it. You all do things on your own time."

Jason tapped the card on her desk. "Thanks for this."

She dipped her chin. "Everything's okay. Nothing I need to worry about, right." There was no question in her tone. She was telling him it should be true.

"Fine." Jason almost stood and then caught himself. That urge to pretend everything was under control would not die. "Well, if you can call having no career in mind, no school plan and a complete inability to cope with failure fine, I guess. Then everything is perfect."

Reyna didn't answer at first. He wasn't sure she *would* answer.

Eventually, she said, "Has it even been a month, Ward? Most people take longer than that to plan a weeklong vacation, much less what they'll do with the rest of their lives. Relax a minute."

Was his mouth hanging open? If it wasn't, it was only because shock had frozen it shut.

"Two years. That's not about getting your body healed." She braced her elbows on the desk and rested her chin on her hands. "That's all mental adjustment. Therapy will help."

Her no-nonsense delivery settled him.

"Thanks for the pep talk." Jason stood and headed for the door.

"You're joking. I get that." Reyna pointed at a doorway in the corner of the open room. "Stick your head in there."

A little nervous, Jason followed her orders. It was an empty office.

Jason stuck his head back out the doorway. "Okay?" What was he supposed to be getting from this?

"That's where the job counselor will be." Reyna had reached the center of the lobby when he walked out of the office. "Soon as I can find one."

"Good." He wasn't alone. There were other people at Concord Court who would need help.

"It's going to be a part-time position. Would leave plenty of hours for going to school." She crossed her arms and tilted her head to the side.

Jason nodded. She seemed to be demanding more of a reaction, but he wasn't sure what they were talking about.

"Think about the job." She raised an eyebrow and held the door open for him. "And next time make an appointment."

Jason followed her orders, walking back out to the pool area, before he realized exactly what she meant. She wanted him to work as a career counselor? He had no training. He didn't even know what kind of job *he* wanted. How could he help other people?

Maybe he should make an appointment to explain that to her.

But he couldn't get his mind off the suggestion, no matter how he worked over his travel writing piece for Angela's class. He'd write a minute and then search for similar job postings to read the required qualifications.

They were all over the place.

When he gave up the homework and web searches, it was dark outside. His informal therapy group should be gathered near the pool. He grabbed his crutch and stepped outside. He reached the gate, and there was no pause in conversation. As he closed the gate behind him, Mira said, "Well, now, look who decided to join us. Where have you been?"

Avoiding you since you learned about my leg because I didn't want to talk about it.

That was the correct answer, but he wasn't going to speak it out loud.

"Here and there. Working on assignments for class. Escorting my mother to whatever event she's picked for the day." Jason took the beer offered and eased down into the empty chair. "What did I miss?"

Marcus answered. "Got a job. I'm pretty happy about that."

"Oh, really? Where?" Jason was interested in this. Law enforcement. Security. Those were the paths a whole lot of people took. That wouldn't work for him. "Are they hiring?"

"Might be hiring, if you want good, hard labor. Got a buddy with a landscaping business. We're going to expand into design, featuring yours truly." He tipped back his beer and drank, his satisfaction with the world clear to see. "Superior Service Lawn and Garden coming at you."

"Does Sawgrass offer degrees in something like that?" Jason decided he needed to get a better look at the class catalog. As he'd searched all afternoon, he'd realized there were a million jobs under the sun. How many could Sawgrass prepare him for?

Marcus shrugged. "Computer-aided design, yes. Landscape design? Nothing that specific, but I've been working with this company ever since I landed here at Concord Court. Did my class project in my final design class. Got a couple of our clients to agree to give me a shot for no charge except cost of the materials." He held out both hands. "Rave reviews, of course. So I made it official, got myself some cards printed and went to the bank to get a small-business loan with the original business as collateral, and now we're going to have offices for meeting with clients in addition to trucks, trailers and mowers. Life is good."

Jason sipped his beer as he made a mental note in case he ever decided to go into business for himself.

Could it be that simple?

"You want a job? You'll start on a mower, but it ain't so bad. Lots of time to think," Marcus added. "We want to work with vets."

The last thing he wanted was more time to think. Jason motioned with his crutch. "Not sure I'm up to the task. I'm still learning how to put one foot in front of the other."

Jason watched all four people at the table pick up their beers and sip.

Almost as if they had opinions on what he'd said, but didn't want to share them. "What?"

Peter Kim shrugged. "It's just…" He put

his beer down. "You can do pretty much anything you want to do, man. Name one thing you literally can't do. I'm not saying the best or even as good as you used to, but can't."

Jason wasn't sure how to answer that.

Mira cleared her throat. "We've seen way worse wounds. You have, too. That can't hold you back." She pointed around the table. "Marcus? He owns his own business. That's a great choice. I'm going to shape young minds and hope they don't maim each other with scalpels in Biology. Wakefield has got his job here, and his cause, training those dogs, for his spare hours. And Peter—"

"I am finishing my first degree so I can go to law school." Peter sighed. "Yes, I'll be forty-four when I start my first year. Is that crazy? Probably. I'm still going to do it because I want to."

"Did you all have the same interests before you enlisted?" Jason asked, his mind on his conversation with Reyna. This would be a good question to start with if he ever had the responsibility of helping other vets find jobs. "I wanted to get out of Rosette. That was my reason. I wanted to see the world."

"The only way to do that was by being shot at?" Sean grunted. "It's okay. I've been there."

Jason stared up at the sky. It was clear, but stars were hard to see. The moon was big and bright.

"What kind of job lets you do that without getting shot at?" Mira asked.

"Pilot," Peter said, "but he's not air force so…"

"You don't get to enjoy anything anyway," Mira said. "You might as well drive the bus here because you'll get to explore as much of those cities that way. Fly in, go to a hotel overnight, fly back out. Local flavor? Only if it's carried in one of the airport shops."

Apparently she'd investigated that option at length.

"How's the writing going?" Mira asked. "Anything there?"

He enjoyed Angela's class, but he wasn't sure it was going well.

"Never make a living at it unless you want to teach." Peter didn't hesitate, just tossed his opinion on writing as a career out in the middle of the conversation. Changing careers hadn't impacted his confidence.

"You would get along well with my mother," Marcus said. "'You'll never have any security if you go into business for yourself.' If she said it once, she said it a hundred times. Could be she's right, but I'll never tell her that. See if I do." This time, his sip of beer was defiant.

Listening to them talk gave Jason the seed of an idea: classes of people hunting for jobs. The brainstorming could help in more ways than one. He glanced around the shadowy table. "My mother insists I need to talk to a therapist. Any of you try that?"

All four of them agreed.

"The counselor Reyna connects you to? She's good, Jason." Sean bent forward, as if he didn't want Jason to miss what he was saying. "All these questions, she can help."

"She might even convince you to talk about whatever happened to land you here." Mira nudged his crutch. "Can't hurt." She paused. "Well, it will hurt, but it's the only way to get over it."

Jason caught the crutch as it toppled toward

him. Was he going to tell them? If he wanted an easy, open door, this was his best shot.

"All the battles I survived. And minor cuts, bruises, burns, all of that—it was scary, but I made it through. When people asked me about the bandage or the scar, I had a good story."

Jason stretched out his right leg and stared hard at the shadow of his missing left foot. "This was due to a car accident. The transfer truck was fired on, swerved and then toppled over. I was pinned under equipment, my leg fractured into a million tiny pieces, and…then a medic got to me, we were transported out, my leg was amputated, my life was saved and completely over all at once. When I woke up here in Miami, my mind was a mess, but there stood my mother. She's been doing her best to put the pieces back together, but I don't want to tell that story over and over. I don't want to see pity. The mad just builds. And then…that look crosses people's faces. Disappointment, I guess, that the story is a lot less exciting and heroic than they expected. I was just doing a job. Somebody asks, and I have to relive the whole thing—the accident, the pain, the fear—but they nod, spew some meaningless words and walk away. Instead of being left alone to deal, I have to tell the same boring thing. Sometimes it seems they don't even care." The angry snap on his final words surprised Jason. "What if, one day, I can't bite back this...anger?"

Marcus shook his head. "What do people expect? We're all saving orphanages when we get hurt?"

Mira sighed. "It's easier to imagine soldiers bringing aid to a village after it's been destroyed than it is them killing the enemy. One's a good story. The other is about war."

No one said anything for the longest time.

Whatever branch they'd served in, active duty and deployments carried a whole lot of similarities, and it was easier to concentrate on the positives than the everyday grind, or worse, the mistakes that led to injuries or lost lives.

"I haven't seen the reactions you're talking about, so I can't be sure," Mira said slowly, as if she were tiptoeing her way through hidden mines, "but I gotta tell you that that's messed up. You didn't die on the field or get injured in the dramatic service that would make a blockbuster movie, but that hard work, day in and out, people deserve to know about that. None of it's easy. Very little of it's safe, even if they want to believe it is. You could have died in that transfer truck and all your mother would have had was a story to tell."

The others at the table were quiet until Sean added, "The problem when you get out is you have too much time to think. While you're in it, you make these brave, stupid, committed decisions, but here, when you're trying to get some sleep, you have all the time in the world to second-guess your choices and replay whatever brought you here. That's enough to bring down the toughest. Whatever I think about Reyna and her management style, she understands our experience and she only works with the best. You don't have to be the toughest. Not anymore."

Sean thumped both feet on the table and stretched back in his chair. "And when you're ready, I can help you find a friend, one with floppy ears and a tail. Watching a dog sleep ain't exciting, but sometimes it'll save your life at three in the morning." The

faint groan that went around the table suggested Sean was a broken record about his
therapy dogs. Jason had to appreciate the
offer anyway.

"That anger, though?" Mira said. "That
will kill you, Ward. Talk to us. Talk to Dr.
Perry. Talk until the infection is gone."

No one else spoke. Mira had said all there
was to say.

"You guys read travel articles?" Jason
asked. The round of "ugh" and "ew" and
"read?" that swept the table made him
chuckle. Okay, so they gave life advice. If
he decided he wanted to try travel writing,
he was on his own. That was fine. "Never
mind."

"You probably won't find dedicated readers
out here, Ward." Reyna Montero stood outside the gate, hands planted on hips. "None
of them chose to read the clearly posted pool
hours. It's been closed for at least two hours.
If only I had an employee around here who
could remind folks about the closing time
for me."

Sean cleared his throat. "We were helping
Ward here. He's still adjusting to life after
service and…" His words trailed off. He

turned to the table, clearly ready for someone to back him up.

Instead, the others stood quietly and made
big shows of moving their chairs silently
back under the table. Mira tapped Jason's
crutch to remind him he needed to follow
suit. If he hadn't watched them file out of the
gate single file like a grade-school field trip
group who had gotten in trouble for being
too rowdy in the museum, he wouldn't have
believed it.

When he tried to walk past Reyna, she
held out a hand and he promptly halted. If
he hadn't needed the crutch, his whole body
would have been at attention, as if he was
dressed in the uniform and trying to pass
inspection.

"Pool closes at ten. I look the other way
because everyone in this group is doing his
or her best to help others. I want you to be
one of those. Bryant was one of the first ten-
ants here. He'll be leaving in a few months.
Someone new will come in. Getting people
to open up and tell their story is hard. Lead-
ers are still needed here, Ward. Don't forget that." She pulled the gate closed. "That
therapist. First visit is no charge. If you like

it, go again. If you hate it, go again. Therapy isn't about fun or liking it or whatever. It's hard and sometimes it's ugly, but when you leave Concord Court, I will know you're going to make it out there. That is my job. I do it well. I'm hoping you'll help me by taking that job offer."

His whole life, Jason had been the guy handing out advice, to his football team in high school, to his crew in the army. Now he kept getting the same answer over and over. He'd run out of road. Time to make an appointment to talk about his feelings.

CHAPTER THIRTEEN

As Jason parked in front of the squat building on the edge of the ring of medical offices surrounding the veterans' hospital,
his phone dinged to tell him he had a text
message. His grade for the Introduction to
Creative Writing class was available for review through the Sawgrass University student portal.

Since he'd only left the final class a little
over thirty minutes ago, his professor must
have had the grades locked and loaded, waiting for the final class's attendance to complete. And she'd had a full classroom.

Angela had stared through him most of
the week, as if he was a mirage holding
down a desk. That answered how open she
was to his apology.

Since he wasn't sure what he'd do after
she accepted his apology, he didn't push the
issue. The only way forward was to tell her

everything, and he wasn't quite ready to get over it if she offered him the usual uneasy clichés about his service.

Their reward for completing the semester had been her thanks and a reading of one of her own poems. It had been about all the different emotions masked by a smile.

"Universal truth, that," Jason muttered as he turned off the ignition. He'd been thinking about it all the way across town.

Well, he'd been thinking about the poem and whether or not he'd get to see a real smile from her, or ever be in that magical spot where a kiss was a second away.

True to her word, she'd given him an A in the class. Four assignments, four uncomfortable turns in the criticism hot seat. "My first A at Sawgrass University. Neither one of us thought it could be done." He stretched in his seat, then decided to snap a picture and text it to his mother. My first college report card, he typed and hit Send.

Then he climbed down out of the truck and realized he hadn't paused, not once, when he made it to the revolving door that led to the ugly lobby. There was no hitch in his step today. It was almost like he and his prosthesis were getting along. Ever since his fall, he'd returned to walking slowly, so carefully. The elevator was waiting on the first floor, so he stepped inside and pushed the button for the third floor. Since this was his second visit, he knew exactly where he was going. Two hours to open all the old wounds. How long would it take until he felt better?

When the doors opened, he made the right turn automatically and opened the door to Michelle Perry's office. His therapist had a nice waiting area, but today the inner door to her office was standing open. When she heard the electronic buzz of the doorbell, she stuck her head around the corner and motioned him in. "I had a cancellation. If you're ready, so am I."

Jason paused in front of the comfy couch. For his first visit to his new therapist, he'd sat there about ten minutes waiting for his appointment. He'd tried to read magazines. Mainly, he'd listened to the ocean wave sounds piped in from somewhere, watched the second hand on the clock move and fidgeted. No time for fidgeting, also known as getting his head right, today.

Instead, he inhaled slowly and exhaled as she shut the door behind him. "Hey, how are you?" he asked. He was uncomfortable, and his skin was too tight, but a polite inquiry worked in a million different situations.

"A little irritated about people who don't show up for their appointments and don't call to cancel, but otherwise," Michelle said with a shrug, "I have no complaints. How are you?"

On his first visit, he'd been struck by how easy the whole thing was. Just talking. No word association or inkblots. He hadn't cried once. Jason wiped his hands on his jeans and sat down, shifting on the cushion to get comfortable. "Fine. Good. Had my last class of the semester today. Got an A. Immediately showed my mother." Wow. Was he seven years old? Running to show off his report card. "After I leave here, I'm going to have a fitting for my new cyborg leg, which will make it possible to run faster and better than I ever did before. Pretty good Wednesday, I guess."

She jotted down a note. For his first visit, he hadn't noticed that, the note-taking. Did that mean he was making progress?

Should he ask? He didn't think so, but his therapist was a lot more comfortable with silence than he'd ever be.

"Okay." She studied his face. "Did you enjoy the class? The last time we talked, you were nervous because you had tried something new and were concerned that the class, and specifically your teacher, would think it was silly. Did they? What was the poet's verdict?" She smoothed her paper, ready to put down more notes, no doubt.

The Poet. She wasn't using it the same way he had, but it had been a while since he'd thought of Angela that way.

"I did enjoy it. No one expected it of me. And listening to the class guess who might have written a kids' book about a spider who was missing a leg was a lot of fun."

"I bet. Why didn't anyone guess it was you?"

"Kinda quiet in class." Jason crossed his arms over his chest. It hadn't bothered him before that no one guessed he was capable of fun and light. Why did it now? "And no one knows about the prosthesis. That would be a dead giveaway."

She raised both eyebrows. "The one that

will be replaced with a 'cyborg leg' later today. No one knows about that? How is that possible after five weeks together?" Her face was perfectly pleasant behind her glasses as she poked hard on the one spot guaranteed to hurt. How did she do that?

"I mean, some people know but..." Jason ran a hand down the nape of his neck and squeezed the tense muscles there. "My mother. My doctors. The woman who runs Concord Court and the group I meet with there." He shrugged. "Why does everyone else have to know?"

She sipped from a mug emblazoned with the phrase "You got this" and then said, "Well, I'm not sure they do, but if you are living your life in a way that keeps your amputation and the reason for it a secret, that is something we should talk about." Then she crossed her hands in her lap to wait.

And she would wait. He could tell by the look in her eyes. His mother had a similar expression when she believed he was being too stubborn for his own good.

For his first visit, his leg had only come up in passing. It was a fact he rattled off, as if it was the state capital of Georgia or the high temperature for the day. He'd covered a lot of ground in that first session with her.

Today would be different. Had she been lulling him into lowering his guard?

"I'm not doing that. I'm not hiding anything." He said it firmly. In his experience, selling half-truths depended on conviction.

She slowly shook her head. She wasn't buying it.

"You aren't hiding it except by making sure no one can see it." She twirled her pen. "Sort of the definition of hiding. Okay, let's talk about school, then. What comes next? Have you planned your fall classes yet?" She waved a hand. "Or you're going to do something else now. You told me your bargain with your mother was only for one class. With that behind you, you're free to make a new choice, right?"

Jason shifted in his seat and realized he was pretty close to fidgeting with an audience. No good.

"That's what I need your help with. I told you that the first day." He had. That had been the only reason he'd come here, to get some guidance from someone who was not his mother.

"Right. Okay." She tapped her pen on the notebook in front of her. "What did you do in the army? That could be valuable experience to your future employer."

"Tactical support. I moved things. Supplies. People. Equipment." Jason shrugged. "Unless I want to be a truck driver, and I don't, not really, I'm not sure it's relevant."

She pursed her lips. "Truck driving could be fun. You'd cover a lot of the country. That's why you enlisted, the chance to explore."

Amazed that she had committed anything he said to memory, Jason braced his elbows on his knees. "And not ever be home. I want to be home for this half of my life." Jason rubbed his forehead, tired of the question mark over his head. "The reason I made it in here was because of my mother's counseling story. I won't be half a world away again when she needs me."

"Makes sense." She made some notes. "Lots of people with military training enter security, police forces or even firefighting."

"No. I promised my mother I'd do something safe." Jason shook his head. "And as easy as it is being a part of that structure, there's the leg."

"Easy, you say. Tell me about that." Her lips turned up in a crocodile smile.

"Following the rules. It's easy. You train. Trust your commander and your team. You learn the protocol. You execute it. Easy. But out here, where there's no real logic to the way things work, that's hard." And it was. If he had to guess, lots of people struggled with that. He couldn't be alone. "On campus? There are groups of kids who play disc golf every day. I don't get that. It's fun, but lots of things are fun. Go and do those, too. You know?" He waited for her to acknowledge his point.

"Definitely, but even here, we have things that give our lives structure. Jobs with certain hours or college courses that meet on these days and times. We have some rules. Pay your rent on the first of the month. Don't try to cross the road unless you're in the crosswalk. Some are laws. Some are expectations. You don't have any trouble with those."

Rolling his eyes in response would be rude. He had a long road to walk with

Michelle Perry, so he wasn't going to be rude this soon. "No problem."

She pointed. "Let's go back farther. High school. Elementary school. What did you want to be?"

Why didn't he have a better answer for this?

"I grew up in a small town. My father was the mayor for most of my life, knew everyone's name and their complaints and never once got frustrated trying to work on them. My mother? She had a good job at the school and led the children's choir at church. So, my father knew every adult in town, and my mother knew every kid. And then there was me. Just me. Everybody in Rosette expected me to be the same, to take the lead, to do the right thing, and I loved them. I did my best. Whenever I messed up, everyone in town made sure my parents knew about it." And no one had hesitated to remind him, either.

"I expect you learned a lot about service and leadership. Those are good qualities." Michelle wrinkled her nose. "But even good qualities can go too far."

"At graduation, my parents would have been happy for me to go out, get a degree and come back to Rosette to be the best accountant the town ever had. That would have been easy." On the wall behind her desk were three certificates. He couldn't read the writing on all of them, but the one in the middle was a recognition of outstanding volunteer service. Next to it was a framed photo of a young woman in dress uniform with people who had to be her parents. Her father wasn't smiling but something about him said pride. Her mother was smiling, but it did nothing to cover the worry on her face.

That reminded him of Angela's poem about what smiles hide.

"I did all the right things. I sang in the church choir," Jason admitted and shook his head. Was he saying it out loud? He'd admitted that once while he and some buddies had been playing cards outside Kandahar and almost never got them to shut up about it. "Team captain. Student council. President of the senior class." He sighed. "Only thing I never managed was the grades. My mother always wanted me to do better than average. She told me I gave up too easily." He didn't want that to be true.

"So, another four years of not quite measuring up sounded like misery then. And the army could give you what you wanted, a chance to get out of Rosette, measurable standards and goals…" She trailed off and raised both eyebrows, waiting because there had to be something more to the answer.

Surely there was. Escaping a perfectly happy childhood made no sense.

"I don't know. In my town and in lots of small towns, if I judge by the stories I've been told, there's an appreciation or a kind of hero worship for servicemen and servicewomen, so it seemed like this noble thing I would be doing. Every small town for a hundred miles had parades to celebrate every holiday, and their veterans marched or rode on floats. That's how I met my first amputee. Got yelled at by my first veteran because of my rudeness. I darted in front of him to grab candy, nearly tripped him. Had a lecture from my mother about the respect we owe veterans. Nearly got a whack from the cane." Jason squeezed his knee. The throb wasn't pain as much as a reminder that there used to be a leg there. "If I joined, I could serve and help people and still do everything I wanted." Jason frowned. Had he even thought it that far out before he enlisted? He'd certainly never imagined being the old soldier limping through a parade.

"Sometimes we have these subconscious pushes that we don't even know are guiding our decisions." Michelle dropped her notebook on the table. "I've known you for a week now, and I see a guy who takes himself pretty seriously, one who is aware of his place in this world and who feels a duty to step up. Forthright. Fair play is important to you. You want to believe in ideals and in justice, and you are prepared to make difficult decisions to accomplish that." She nodded. "Tell me where I'm wrong."

Jason stretched again, uncomfortable with every bit of what she'd said. "I'm a guy who is completely out of touch with this world."

"No way. I know lots of people like you. I talk to them every day, men and women who signed up to serve. That's why I love what I do. Some people," she said and dipped her chin down to make sure he knew she was talking about him, "believe that only broken people come to therapy, but I am telling you, the soldiers and sailors and marines and airmen and airwomen that come in here? They are ready to be stronger than they've ever been. All they need, and all you need, is to deal with the weak spots. You aren't broken. That wound? The one that led to the amputation and the one that's keeping you from moving forward, that's it. That's all you have to overcome. When you remember how far around the world you've been, this is the same as turning into your driveway. You are so close, Jason. You can do this."

Jason blinked as he absorbed her speech. "I'm guessing you understand what you're talking about. You were army, too."

"I was. And that's why I'll volunteer my time with Concord Court until Reyna tells me to go away. This world needs people who believe in justice and service, even if they have wounds that have to be healed first." She tilted her head. "Maybe that's it," she said slowly.

More nervous than he had been since he set foot in her office the first day, Jason cleared his throat. He'd ask what she meant, but she was going to tell him anyway. She'd picked up her notebook, so whatever it was, it would be a doozy.

"You don't believe you're a hero." She studied him closely. "Do you?"

His first reaction was to shake his head firmly. "No. I did a job."

"When you were a kid in Rosette and you watched veterans come home to parades, you knew they were heroes." Patience settled on her face again. He didn't care for it.

"Yes," he snapped. "It's not the same thing."

"Because you were doing what was expected of you while they…" She shrugged. "I don't get it."

Jason closed his eyes. Was he going to say this out loud? "I lost my leg because of a car accident. My transfer truck crashed. There's nothing heroic about being in the wrong place at the wrong time. I could have done that in Rosette." Before she could respond, he added, "You know how my mother got me here? She told me about her own experience with therapy when grief over my father's death made her miserable. I wasn't there for her. I'm not a hero. I'm a guy who messes up. Sometimes."

"You love your mother. The truth is, you might not have seen her grief if you'd been here and you might not have been able to help anyway. You were doing the job you were trained for. There are a lot of people too afraid to step into the gap and you did it. Whether an enemy combatant caused your injury or not, you were hurt in the service of your country and the others you served with. I'm asking you, if another soldier were telling you this and feeling less than he should because his injury came from an accident instead of an enemy shot, what would you say to him?"

Jason crossed his arms over his chest. What would he say?

"Every job matters. Every person in the crew matters." Jason rubbed his forehead. "I said it every day to the guys I worked with and who trusted me and I knew it was true. It takes every man and woman to accomplish the objective, wherever they serve." Some of the tension left his shoulders. "I wouldn't let a guy who'd nearly been killed in an accident following my orders wonder for one second if his life mattered less than another one who was shot in battle. Not for one second."

The way Michelle bugged her eyes out made him laugh. Maybe it was time to roll his eyes when he wanted to. She wasn't holding back.

"Don't let yourself imagine for one second that your sacrifice is less important, either. Thank you for making my point for me." She pointed at him. "I love it when that happens."

"And you only had to lead me there by the hand and stand on my shoelaces to make me stop long enough to say it."

She shrugged her shoulder. "It's what I do. The training kicks in and everything falls into place."

Jason laughed. He'd expected lots of probing questions that turned into issues with a capital *I*, not laughter. But he was going to walk out of here better.

"You told me about the old guy at the parade when we first met, too. His reaction, his wound stuck with you. Maybe because you were young or even then knew that war was dangerous, life and death. It's a scary thing." She pointed her pen at him. "Imagine if another man with a similar wound had used the opportunity to talk to you about his experience. Would your life have turned out differently? This injury wouldn't slow you down. You could be that guy for others. You will be that guy, the one who shows life goes on and gets better. I have no doubt."

Jason straightened in his seat. An almost stranger believed he could lead others.

"You want to serve. You have valuable experience that can help many vets. You can write." She tapped her pen again. "And school... Well, you're on the fence about that. Counseling. You could be good at this or at leading groups returning, but you'd need some training. Sawgrass has a great social work program." Then she chuckled. "Reyna called me this morning to talk about her need for a career counselor. Have the two of you chatted about that job? She's so good at pulling all the strings together."

Jason scrubbed a hand over his face. "Yes. And I've worn out my fingers searching for information on how that would even work. I don't have a counseling or social work degree."

"Okay, but our concept, mine and Reyna's, was that I would run the program, but we'd have someone on hand to facilitate groups, and help with web searches and applications. This could be great for you and for every vet at Concord." She scribbled a note on a piece of paper. "Here's the professor you should talk to at Sawgrass. He's head of the department over there, and he can give you some direction about what an undergraduate degree in social work can take and where you can go with it. He's on board to help us find government and nonprofit support programs, so he knows all about this project."

Reyna would make this plan happen, and her plan included him. Since every time he met Reyna Montero, she was conquering each step with a firm expression on her face, he was pretty sure she could do anything she set her mind to.

Except keep the pool group away from the pool.

He checked the clock. He'd nearly run out his hour. A little career talk but nothing that hurt. Good visit.

"And this new prosthesis," Michelle drawled. "How is that going to change your life?" She waved a hand at the clock. "We started early. We have more time."

Jason swallowed his sigh.

"It will allow me to run. Basically, I will

run faster and better than I ever have." Jason shrugged. "Cyborg."

"Have you missed running?" She reached over to pick up the notebook again. Clearly they were in new therapy territory.

"Missed it? I wouldn't say that. It's hotter than the face of the sun out there. Running isn't a joy for me. It never has been." Jason stretched his leg. "But it helps. Gets me out of my head, you know?"

She nodded. "Tell me about this cyborg leg."

"You've seen something similar. It's metal, designed with a special curve to give each step extra power. Apparently, it's the tip of the iceberg. I can change my leg according to my mood, as long as the money holds out. Be better than I ever was with both feet."

"I've seen them. There's no way to hide that, Jason. People will see your prosthesis. They will ask you about your amputation and your service and all of that stuff you've been avoiding." She picked up her mug. "Are you ready for that?"

He looked down at his left leg. Today, no one would know he was any different. He was wearing jeans and running shoes and he'd walked into this building without a single hitch in his step. Learning to run on his new leg wouldn't be as easy.

"I don't know, but I'll have to get there." He exhaled loudly. "Do you ever get so sick of the conversation that runs on a loop in your head? I can't sleep at night because I'm telling myself I have to get over all of it and then I'm worried I'll never be over it, that I'm stuck in this weird limbo forever. Running will help with that. I've got to learn how."

Michelle agreed. "Yes, you do. You will. And it's going to go smoother than you imagine. You are also going to run into people who ask dumb questions. Kids will stare and point. You will be reminded that you aren't the same as you were before. There will be days when the leg fails you because all bodies do that, but more often than all that, you are going to run. You are going to run and sweat and leave all that worry behind for however long you run. You know this. Having this new prosthesis made is the proof of exactly what I said, you know. You aren't broken. This isn't easy. It wouldn't be easy for anyone, but you can do this because you want to do this." She narrowed her eyes at him. "And you better have news to report when I see you next. Let's drop it to once a week."

He should tell her about falling and the immediate rage and fear that had swamped him.

But she was offering him an open door.

Relieved, Jason asked, "Is that because I'm doing so well?"

"It's because you need some time to make progress on your own." Michelle stood up. "Find out about social work, try running on your new leg." She pursed her lips. "The third thing… What was the third thing?" She studied the ceiling. "Oh, you should also tell someone about your leg, someone who doesn't know but might want to."

Immediately, the image of Angela Simmons's face popped up.

Michelle studied him. "As soon as I said it, you pictured someone. Is it a female someone?"

"Why would you think that?" Jason asked. He tried for innocent, but he'd never been all that good at pulling it off.

"Your history. Your work. What you want for your future." She sniffed. "We've sort of hit on all the pieces this week. There's more to do, obviously, but the only thing I didn't hear was a relationship. You told me you're single. Next time, I want to find out more about that." She wrinkled her nose. "But whoever she is, you should tell her. Ask her out. Whatever. Life is short." She held up her hand and wiggled her fingers so that light bounced off the diamond on her finger. "I'm a fan of the happy relationship."

Jason stood. "Well, there was someone, but I…"

Michelle crossed her arms over her chest, her eyes locked on his. "But you…"

"But I fell. We were dancing and I fell, and instead of laughing it off like a normal, well-adjusted human, I had this…" Was he going to admit this? It was the worst part. "I kept it locked down, but I was angry and frustrated and ashamed, so I escaped. Ran away. No one needs to deal with even one of those emotions, much less all three or how-ever many were in that swamp." He'd never taken his own problems out on others. This amputation was no reason to start.

"Emotions are normal things, Jason. How you handle them is the difference. We'll talk about that. Anger. It's logical here, isn't it? Only your response to it matters. You discuss it here, with the group around the pool, with the people who matter, and you raise your odds of making only the right decisions." Michelle narrowed her eyes. "But it wasn't Reyna you pictured. She already knows about your amputation. Somebody else, and she's different than your usual type. You didn't meet her in a bar."

Jason cleared his throat. "I don't have a type, although bars are good for lots of things. I meet people."

"At school." Michelle stared into the distance. "Oh. She's a professor." She clasped her hands together. "Wednesday, same time. I want to know more."

Jason held up a hand and opened the door. It was a good thing her next appointment was already chilling on the couch because he might have stopped to protest that she didn't know what she was talking about.

But she did. And if he figured out why his sudden turn of luck was surrounded on all sides by women who were too smart for his own good, he might make a change.

Probably not, but sometimes a man needed to be dumb and unhappy. All this enlightenment was moving too quickly for him.

CHAPTER FOURTEEN

ON SATURDAY, ANGELA was stretched out in the hammock she and Greer had hung about two seconds after she closed on her house. The phone was perched on her shoulder while she held a notebook with one hand and did her best to draw a cute spider with only seven legs. It was no problem to get the legs right. The "cute" part was giving her trouble. Since she was supposed to be jotting down ideas for poems, not doing bad doodles of circles with hairy legs, she ignored the notebook to focus on her daughter.

"So, the nursery is almost finished. How did the doctor visit go? Did you get to see the baby on a sonogram?" Angela asked. Greer's phone calls that week had all been rushed because her work schedule was disjointed. She'd gone with Kate to the doctor, a fact that Angela had done her best not to dwell on. Greer was going to have a life that had nothing to do with her eventually. She was getting an early start on it.

"I did, and they decided to find out. They're having a boy," Greer said in a breathless rush. "Everyone is pretty excited."

Rodney most of all. He'd dreamed of having a son since the day he and Angela got engaged. "That's great, baby. You'll have a little brother. That's awesome."

"Yeah." Whatever was on her mind would trickle out.

Angela dropped a foot to the porch below her and gave the hammock a nudge. It was almost too hot for this. Early morning was the only time she could stand to be outside in the Florida heat. Pretty soon, only air-conditioning would do.

"It's just that…" Greer sighed. "By the time he's any fun, I'll be away at school. Far away. Unless I change all my plans."

Angela closed her eyes to enjoy the cool breeze stirred up by the sway of the hammock. "G, listen. You're going to be a great big sister. Even if you go to college on the East Coast, you'll see him on holidays and during the summer and you'll call and you'll text and all the things we're doing. It's a challenge, but you can love your little brother from Harvard or Yale or wherever you decide to go."

Angela stared at the circles dotting the page of her notebook and turned back to the poem she'd come out here to work on. It was a blurry mess about distance that she needed to tighten up. At her own unintended pun, Angela tossed the notebook on the porch under the hammock. Obviously, she was not a good poet that day.

"I know. I also know it's not the same." Greer's quiet voice sharpened Angela's focus.

This was it. This was the thing that was growing between them this summer that neither one of them wanted to let get out of hand.

"It's not." Angela studied the spot on the underside of her porch that needed a fresh coat of paint. "But you have a plan for your life. You've always had a plan." The girl had ordered her stuffed animals by color and age before she'd started first grade. "Only you know when you can change that. The education you've always wanted is worth hard work, even if it's work you do to make sure your little brother knows you instead of studying."

Angela closed her eyes. "But there's a good education available there in Nashville, other choices in Tennessee, and so many within a half day's drive that would mean you could go home when you needed to." She ought to know. She'd done a thorough study of all those options before she'd landed at Sawgrass. Those big names? Yeah, they didn't hire often and they certainly didn't recruit the way Sawgrass had. What if she'd been able to make one of those choices work?

"I don't have to decide today. The senator says he's not so sure Ivy is the option to go for anymore. He says they cost too much for too little return. I could go to a state school for half the price and land a good job easily."

Angela wasn't sure what to read into Greer's tone. The senator's advice was good and important, clearly. But what about her mother?

"And what does Dad say? Have you talked about this with him?" Angela asked and tried to roll up and out of the hammock without grunting. For this conversation, she needed to move.

"It's up to me. Like everything else has been since you guys got divorced, my whole life and every decision is up to me," Greer snapped. "I'm so tired of getting that answer. 'It's up to you.' I'm asking for advice and I can't get any."

Angela bit her lip and refused to mention that this had always been Rodney Simmons's route for as long as she'd known him. He couldn't give advice, but he could certainly tell you where you'd gone wrong after everything was over.

It was easy to point the finger at Rodney, but Greer's frustration was with them both.

"That's because you're a smart girl." And she was going to do what she'd always done for Rodney: fill in the blanks. Every time he'd refused to make a decision or held back the words she wanted, she'd supplied them. "He loves you and only wants the best for you. Unfortunately, only you know the best for you. I hope you'll keep the Ivies in your sights, because that's always been your dream. Your dad's life is changing, and you're a part of that, but this is a piece that belongs only to you."

Angela thumped her head against the porch post and wondered if she was saying the wrong things.

"Thanks, Mom. It's because everything is baby, baby, baby here, all the time baby, that I'm too wrapped up in it. Today, Dad and Kate want to have engagement photos taken. I thought that was what they did in front of the Eiffel Tower without me, but no, this is something *official*. That was to share the news with their friends and family. And rub it in, but whatever, they're lovebirds." Greer grumbled under her breath for a minute. "So, anyway, I'm getting ready to have my status as third wheel solidified forever by being in a formal photo with them."

The bittersweet pleasure of listening to her daughter talk like an almost-seventeen-year-old from hours away was hard to swallow. She was growing up and Angela was missing it.

"What are you doing today?" Greer asked.

"Trying to write. It's not going well." Angela refused to think of her badly drawn spiders. "Not well" really didn't capture the mood. It had been more than a full week since the grades had been turned in and… nothing. Not a word from Jason Ward. She'd spent time in her office, finalizing files for the summer semester and preparing notes for the staff meeting she'd planned the next week. His mother had her phone number. He could find her if he wanted.

She'd spent way too much time thinking that same thing.

"Some days you need a change of scenery. Isn't that what you told me when I was buried under that paper on Shakespeare, who has to be the worst writer that we are forced to study. I mean, what is the point of Romeo or Juliet? It's dumb."

Angela rubbed the sudden pain in the middle of her chest. "It's a good thing you are so far away or we would have to have a serious heart-to-heart conversation about your language. Shakespeare wrote whole plays in rhyme. Don't tell me that's not impressive. Do you know how many words he made up? I mean, give the dead guy some respect, at least when you are talking to your mother, who spends a lot of time trying to convince other students to do the same."

"Making up new words is your measure of greatness? Pretty sure any toddler can do that." Greer was laughing. They'd had this conversation a hundred times.

"And if you think he's bad, let me introduce you to Hemingway." Angela enjoyed adding that, mainly as a dig at her ex-husband and his preferences, but also because she'd hated every minute of *For Whom the Bell Tolls* and would never torture children with it in her classroom.

"Yeah, yeah, but you'll be on the tour of his house when we hit Key West because we are doing that."

Angela was relieved. "We are doing it. It's a date, you and me."

Greer's giggles were reassuring. She'd started out entirely too quiet. Now she might as well be six instead of sixteen. This baby brother was a blessing. If it caused Greer to evaluate her plans now, Angela would be certain Greer was doing exactly what she wanted when she went to college, instead of being carried along on daydreams of being a lawyer. When she was little, Greer had relished being able to shout, "I object." She was old enough now to know that there was so much more to being a lawyer than court-room drama.

"I love you, Mom. I wish we were together today." In the blink of an eye, Greer was almost an adult again. What a roller coaster sixteen-going-on-seventeen could be.

Blinking back tears, Angela reminded herself that the roller coaster was a long one. Even for forty-and-a-little-bit-extra.

"I'm proud of you, Greer. Now go get ready. Tell your Dad I got my invitation and my RSVP card is in the mail." Angela had made sure to put a floral stamp on it, in honor of her ex-husband's literary style. Not that he would notice. This was the lowest level of petty, but Angela wasn't ready to give it up.

"Did you include a plus-one?" Greer asked immediately. She didn't even have to pause to come up with the question. As soon as Angela stopped talking, Greer fired back with her question, as if that was right there, at the front of her concerns about this wedding. Angela had hoped that her daughter would get the picture and come to understand that the plus-one wasn't all that important in the big scheme of things, the long, winding road that was life.

But no. Her practical daughter had one romantic hotspot: dates to weddings, especially as they concerned her mother.

"I did not." She'd been tempted to.

"Don't miss out on the captain," Greer ordered. There was clapping in the background of the call. Either her daughter had learned how to clap with one hand or... Angela couldn't come up with another option. "Stop waiting. Kate said he definitely wants you to call. It's not the same as when you were young, Mom."

Kate said. Ouch. Another expert to knock "Mother knows best" out of the running.

The "young" part was a direct hit, too. In her own mind, she was still young. Would Greer agree?

"Even in the dark ages, when cell phones were new and rare, we could call them, G." Annoyed at how difficult standing her high ground with her daughter had gotten, Angela added, "When I decide it's time to date, I'll do it because I want to, not because of some artificial deadline or the overwhelming peer pressure I'm experiencing."

"Right." Greer's flat tone communicated her disappointment.

"Make sure your father knows I don't intend to bring anyone—that will make his penny-pinching heart content. I don't want to hear another word about the budget for his destination wedding." Angela shook her head. This was what she wasn't going to do—she would not drag Greer in between them. "Forget I said that. It's nice of them to include me. I can't wait to spend time with you, my favorite person in the world."

"I just wish…" Greer huffed out a breath. "Dad is totally gross with how ecstatic he is about this baby. I wish you were really happy."

"What? I am!" Angela laughed. "Get off the phone." She was. What was the problem? Why was she having to defend her happiness over and over?

Greer said, "I will, but you gotta know I still have my fingers crossed for a guy, someone who makes everything in your life, all the good things you have, great, Mom. It's not really wrong to want that, too. Is it?"

Angela winced. This was an easier lecture when Greer was drawing castles and

princes. Even then, her girl had been determined to be the one on the horse with the
sword. "Of course not, baby. It makes perfect sense to want that, but not to rearrange
your life, your goals, your plans in case it
might happen someday. If that man shows
up while I'm out there, doing my thing,
great. I'll ask him to your father's wedding."

Greer snorted. "Not after the guest list
is set and budgeted accordingly, you better not."

Relieved, Angela said, "He'd just get in
the way of our trip to Hemingway's house.
Whoever he is, he probably doesn't even like
cats."

"Or he's the world's second biggest fan
of war stories and bull fights. Then what?"
Greer asked.

"Impossible. There cannot be two."
Angela closed her eyes to wipe away the
thought of spending any time with another
Hemingway fan.

"Love you." Greer waited for Angela to
say the same and the call was ended.

Angela picked up the notebook and
frowned at the ugly spiders she'd drawn.
They were still better than Jason's. She'd

planned to give him the name of someone in the graphic arts area at Sawgrass. A real artist could help him. It was a cute story. She didn't know much about kids' literature, but there might be something there.

But Jason had done a good job of never being in the same place she was. She'd even gone to the beach closest to Sawgrass on a nice Wednesday afternoon on the off chance that he or his mother might have chosen that day to explore the same spot. It had worked when she wasn't trying to find him. When she wanted to run into Jason? No way.

She could call him. That was easy. She had the perfect excuse.

Then she was reminded that he'd taken the high road with their selfie and told her she'd have to ask for his number if she wanted it. She hadn't asked.

What did it mean that he hadn't gotten hers, either? Maybe he wasn't really interested in anything more than conversation whenever they ran into each other.

Angela could call his mother, suggest they meet somewhere for something and hope he came along. Mae had insisted Angela have her phone number in case the urge to try something as exciting as parasailing or brunch hit. She and Jason could find a bench somewhere while his mother jumped out of an airplane or something. Not quite as easy but not totally unreasonable.

Or she could regress to high school and drive by his house to see if he was home, freak out if he was and drive off in a panic or mope around the house if he wasn't because he'd found a much better way to spend his time. That was the worst option.

She wanted to see him. It had been a long time since she'd felt this way.

And she was picking up her car keys before she could explain to herself that she was entirely too old for ridiculous crush shenanigans.

It was a beautiful day for a drive and Concord Court was less than ten minutes from her bungalow, so she enjoyed the leisurely drive as she carefully navigated the hordes of people on bicycles. Some were wearing training gear and spandex; others were twelve and had baskets on the fronts of their bikes. All of them had blinking red safety lights on the seats, which reminded her of the first time she and Jason had talked on a bench.

She was singing along with the radio as she spotted a group of runners. In the sea of extreme fitness, they stood out because they had no wheels. Just pumping arms and really nice muscles in tan, strong backs covered in sweat. She slowed down to a crawl because of safety, obviously. The fact that it was nice to watch them run was a bonus. They turned into the driveway of Concord Court ahead of her and she realized the runner at the front of the group, the one setting the pace, was Mira, the student she'd told Jason about. And as they slowed and spread out to trickle over to the sidewalk in front of a beautiful pool, she could see that one of the runners was wearing a prosthesis, the metal kind that serious athletes wore. She'd never seen one in real life, just in pictures. It hadn't slowed this guy down a bit.

She turned away toward the back of the property and did her best not to tense up when she saw Jason's big red truck parked in front of the nearest building. Home. He was home. Good to know? Maybe? What was she doing here?

Angela dug her cell phone out of her purse and turned it over and over while she evaluated her choices. She scrolled through her contacts and found Mae Ward.

"What do I say?" Angela muttered. *Hi. I'm outside your son's house.* Nothing reasonable came to mind. Either she was losing her grip on words, which would be concerning since she'd centered her whole life around them, or this was a terrible plan. Half a second from reversing out of the spot, she glanced out her window to see one of the joggers walking toward her. This was where panic should set in.

Then he got close enough and she recognized his face. Jason. And he was the one with the prosthesis.

A dozen different puzzle pieces all clicked into line to make a new picture.

Was this the secret he'd been holding on to?

"Hey, J, wait up!"

Mira Peters was jogging down the sidewalk.

It was a bright, sunny July day, not a storm cloud in sight.

The lightning bolt struck anyway.

He hadn't called because he was dating someone else.

And he'd had no trouble telling Mira about his amputation, so it was clear she was a better choice for him.

Escape.

That was what she needed and right now, even though Jason had turned to glance at Mira.

The only thing weirder than finding your creative writing professor parked outside your house would have to be watching her burn rubber out of the parking lot without giving any explanation.

Fine. She'd roll down her window, spit out her advice on the graphic artist, lie through her teeth about some fabulous adventure that she had to get to immediately and drive sedately away. Almost like a normal person.

She could manage that.

CHAPTER FIFTEEN

GETTING UP TO run had been a real struggle that Saturday morning, but Jason knew he'd done the right thing when they jogged into the parking lot at Concord Court. He'd worn the prosthesis for one training run, but today was his first attempt in the real world. And he'd made it.

Even though he'd been scared he would hold the rest of the group back, he'd finished the run. He knew Mira had shortened the distance, and she'd kept the pace steady but slow for him. In the beginning, he'd almost dropped out. He wasn't going to be the weight for this team. They weren't training for anything specific, still, they were a team. Then Marcus and Peter had dropped behind him, leaving him solidly in the middle. If he faltered, they'd catch him. He'd done the same for others throughout a long military career. Now, when he needed support, they'd stepped up. He'd been determined to make this run count.

He'd never been so glad to see Concord Court in his life, but he'd done it.

And not one of his team had said a thing about it. Whether they had doubts or not, they expected him to make it.

That was the way it should be. Without the prosthesis, no one would have patted his head for completing an easy run. He didn't want any special treatment that morning, either.

The only words spoken had come from Sean. "Same time tomorrow?" Then they'd all dispersed.

Jason's knee burned. Sweat dampened his hair. Sunburn was tickling along the tops of his shoulders and across the bridge of his nose, but he was more himself than he had been in a while.

And then he saw the car parked next to his and recognized the driver.

Angela was here, watching him. The shock on her face was pretty much what he'd expected when he'd stepped outside to run with the group for the first time. Training at his prosthetist's office had been easy enough. He'd worked with the leg and had a few adjustments made, and he'd run and run on the never-ending treadmill. The comfortable, reliable surface and the power of his new leg had given him a boost of confidence.

When he'd fallen in with Mira, Sean, Marcus and Peter, he'd done so silently. If they'd been shocked by the appearance of his leg, they hadn't said a thing. He hadn't asked. He'd put his head down, and he'd started to run. Keeping up after so long out of the game had taken every bit of energy he had.

Angela's shock was hard to ignore.

With Mira calling him, he was glad to have the chance to turn away. Otherwise, he and Angela might have been locked in a staring contest until heatstroke did them both in.

"Yeah?" he asked as he pulled his soaked T-shirt off his shoulders. At some point, he'd acclimate to the heat and humidity, but right now, southern Florida was a test.

"I wanted to say thanks for joining us. Usually, I have to nag those guys to show up, but once they knew you'd be here, they were all grins and happy Saturday vibes."

She wiped wet strands of hair away from her face and then shook her finger. "You have to keep running. I don't know how long the good mood will last, but it's so much easier when I don't have to drag any dead weight, too."

Jason dipped his chin down. "Really? You're telling me that today was a positive, happy run?" He hadn't heard any complaints, but even the worst run could be tolerated for the right reason. That sometimes happened when the crew knew someone needed them. And he'd needed his new crew today.

"Yes. You see what I mean?" She tilted her head down and mirrored his stance. "Would I lie to you?"

"In a heartbeat, but thanks." He grinned and squeezed her shoulder. "I needed all of it. Stepping out with the leg will get easier. It's nice to have you with me right now."

She stared down at it, and he braced himself. Whatever she said, it would be well intended, even if it punched a hole in his wispy confidence. "Honestly, it's part of you, just like any other. Anybody disagrees, you send them to me."

"I can take care of myself, but thank you.

No need to throw a punch on my behalf."
Jason checked on Angela's car. She hadn't
moved. She'd closed her mouth, so she was
no longer caught midgasp, but he still had
no idea what she was thinking.

"No punches. More like education. I could
give a lesson on how evolution changes de-
fense systems to prepare for new conditions.
This is sort of the same. You're adapting and
you'll come out stronger on the other side
because of it." She casually shot a side-eye
at Angela. "What's that about? Is it juicy?
I like juicy."

Jason laughed. "I'm not sure."

"You'll let me know, though, if it's something good, right? I live for this kind of
stuff." Mira had tangled her fingers together
under her chin to beg.

"I most definitely will not tell you anything, especially if it's juicy." Jason shook
his head as her face fell. Mira narrowed her
eyes at him and then headed for the parked
car. "Hey, Dr. Simmons, how are you? Long
time, no see."

Angela shoved her sunglasses to the top
of her head. "I'm doing well, Mira. Out on
my way to a tourist trap, and I remembered

Jason was here. I wanted to give him the name of a graphic artist who might be able to help him with his kids' book. The story he wrote is adorable, but his drawing…" Angela wrinkled her nose. "I guess you saw it, though. You know what I'm talking about. Still, it's a writing class, not a drawing one, so I was impressed he gave it a shot."

Mira sent him a sideways glance, but he had no hints to give her. Why would he be showing off his creative writing assignment?

"No, he hasn't shared any of his writing with us. We talked about the class. I told him he definitely needed to get his work into the literary magazine. I'm going to be a science teacher, but my mother singlehandedly covered the first print run when my poem came out. When the aliens arrive, they'll be finding copies of that edition of the magazine all over the world. Every auntie in all four corners of the globe got multiples."

Angela smiled and Jason remembered how much he enjoyed seeing that. Now that he'd seen shock, he realized how much he needed that smile.

"Fame is something we all have to learn to cope with, Mira. I'm glad your mother spread the word." She braced her arm on the car door and then leaned back quickly.

"Well, I should be going. It's my second cousin's birthday, and we're all headed out to the arcade to celebrate this afternoon." Mira pinched her tank top and pulled it away. "A shower is required." Then she raised a hand to wave goodbye and jogged down the sidewalk. Jason wasn't certain which townhouse was hers, but she was on the north side of the property somewhere.

Angela watched her go for entirely too long. Was she killing time? He clenched his shirt in one hand and crossed his arms over his chest. Whatever came next, it was her move now.

"Want to tell me what you're doing here?" Jason asked. "I got the impression you didn't have much to say to me after our dance." His story had been his attempt at an apology. Had she gotten that?

Eventually she shifted back to face him. "I guess I wasn't sure what to say since I didn't know what the problem was, Jason." She shot a quick glance down at his prosthesis. Obviously they were now on the same page. "Owen Langford. He's the professor who teaches several graphic arts classes. At least one of them focuses on computer-aided animation. If there's something to your story, you need better illustrations. He could help. That's all. I don't know if you want to go any further with your writing, but you'll need better graphics. He can at least connect you to a student who needs an easy class project. You might get cute spiders for free that way." She faced the steering wheel. "So, that's it. Glad I ran into you. Gotta run."

She started to roll her window up. Taking a chance, Jason stepped closer to her car and put his hand on the window. Lucky for him, she stopped it before it mashed his fingers. "That's what you came here to tell me? It had nothing to do with your promise to my mother to convince me to give parasailing a try? Now you obviously understand why you're doomed with that promise."

She snorted. "What? No way. You were *never* interested in going with me." She motioned with a weird wave. "And I get it. Everything has changed."

What did that mean? The only thing that was different was now she knew about his amputation.

Which might explain why he couldn't be the guy she needed him to be.

Not anymore.

"Come inside. I do need a shower and to get off this leg, but we can talk after." He wanted to plant himself in her path and refuse to move, but the burn on his knee was building. Time to sit.

She immediately shook her head. "Uh, no, I've got a tour lined up. It cost a pretty penny, so I can't miss it. I've got to go."

Had she come by to invite him with her? Man, he wanted that to be the truth.

Deciding to ignore her shocked expression when she'd seen the leg, Jason asked, "What time is the tour?"

Hard to wiggle out of a direct question.

Her eyes darted to the side. Would she lie to him? "Three?" Her answer was definitely a question.

"It's not quite noon. Come on in." Jason motioned over his shoulder as he turned to unlock his front door. She'd follow him or she wouldn't. He needed to know the answer.

When he heard the car door shut behind him, some of the worry eased. However she felt about his leg, the conversation wasn't quite over yet.

"Want something to drink?" Jason asked as he let her in. "Water is your only choice, but I have plenty of it." He padded into the kitchen to open the refrigerator, more at ease with Angela than he'd expected. Of course, she'd kept her attention turned firmly away from him every second they'd been together. Not a great sign.

"I didn't come to interrupt your Saturday plans," Angela said. Her voice was loud, as if she was covering for nerves by turning everything up in volume.

When she took the bottle from him, he pointed at the hallway. "Here's my only plan for now. Me. Shower. Can you wait ten minutes?"

She finally nodded, so he hurried into the bathroom, removed the prosthesis and eased into the hot shower. Concord Court had a lot of good amenities. Their walk-in showers with immediate hot water and comfortable benches? Yeah, he'd been converted. Before his time here, he'd expected only fancy people required a seat in the shower. Now he knew it was the only way to live. He could sit and clear his mind. Today, there was only one thing, one person, on his mind.

After a quick towel dry, he grabbed a crutch and found some dry clothes. Before he left his bedroom, he studied his prosthesis. Should he put it back on?

Maybe this was the best way to have a real conversation. He'd yank off the bandages, so to speak, and let the chips fall and throw in another cliché for good measure.

If he'd been left to his own devices in someone's home for the first time, he might have found good opportunity to study their movie collection or music or anything that was on display. His home had none of that. He'd never seen the reason to build large collections of stuff that would have to follow him wherever he went. But it was time to start building.

There were two pictures on the bookcases flanking the large-screen television. One was of his graduation day from basic training, his father beaming and his mother worried behind a big smile like the one he'd seen in Michelle's office. The other was a baby picture his mother had given him. She was certain a home without photos was a hotel in disguise, so she'd given him a picture of the two of them at his second birthday party. He was wearing a party hat, but it was listing sideways as if he'd had too much juice to drink.

"You were a cute little boy." Angela tapped the photo. "I have a picture like that of Greer, too. She hated having that hat on crooked and would repeat 'ficit, ficit' until I fixed it. Bossy. We should have guessed she'd grow up to be a lawyer."

"A gift from my mother. Every time she comes over, she brings something else. The first day, it was the couch, so I'm glad her gifts are getting smaller." Jason paused behind her and wondered what he should say to get the right conversation rolling. He wanted to demand to know what she thought about his leg or for her to ask all the questions he dreaded or to tell him what she wanted.

All of that was hard. He could pretend he believed she had something planned this afternoon and let them both off the hook.

"Thanks for the recommendation. For the artist. I don't have any plans to go any further with the book, but it could be a cool gift, something to give back to my mother when she makes good on her threat to deliver all my high school yearbooks here. I don't know why she kept them in the first place, but I'm sure she wants them out of her retirement sanctuary."

Jason pointed at the couch. "Do you have time to sit?" He leaned against the crutch and waited. He'd let her pick the direction.

"Sorry to keep you standing," she muttered and dropped down on the sofa, guilt flickering across her face before she wiped it away.

Sorry. As if she was causing the amputee an imposition by rudely standing in his presence?

Irritation set his jaw. That was a glimmer of the worst-case scenario, that guilt over inconveniencing him.

Angela nervously cleared her throat. "Kids' story. That's the first time any student has turned one in. I'm not sure it really met my grading criteria, but you definitely deserve points for creativity." She ran a hand over her forehead. "How did you come up with the story?"

"A spider who is missing a leg and knocks over everything in his path?" Jason grunted as he sat down and caught the crutch before it hit the lamp on the table beside him. The shower had helped with the irritated skin, but the throb was still there. "Hard to say where the inspiration came from."

He thought she would smile, but she didn't.

"Talking about my amputation is hard for me, so I don't do it any more than I have to. Dancing is pretty much the same, because the chance that I'll fall is better than even odds. I'm sorry you were there to see it. The spider story is a kind of apology." Jason rubbed his knee until he saw the way her eyes were locked to his hand. Drawing attention to his amputation was not the way to go.

"I'd like to know more." Angela crossed her arms over her chest. "If you'll tell me."

He liked how she phrased the request. His answer was his choice alone.

"Tactical support. That was my job in the army. Basically, I moved things. There was nothing all that glamorous about it, but wars run on supplies."

When she nodded her understanding, he relaxed a fraction. She wasn't bored. She wasn't asking questions to fill the silence. She wasn't making him into super soldier. Angela was waiting for his story.

"There's no big battle that I won or life that I saved. The truck that I was in crashed after we were fired on and equipment smashed my lower left leg into bits. The only way to save my life was to amputate." Jason scrubbed a hand over his face. "I've been trying to put my life back together again ever since. Landed here in Miami with my mother for a nurse. Enrolled at Sawgrass. You know the rest."

Angela stared hard at her knees for a long minute. "Where were you?"

Jason braced himself. "Afghanistan."

She nodded again. "Okay."

Jason studied her. He didn't see curiosity or worry or fear or anything.

Then a loud sniffle ripped through the quiet room, and she pinched her nose closed. Was she crying?

"Sorry. I'm just so glad you're here." Then she blinked rapidly. "If you ever want to tell me more, you can. I know it's a lot to carry, and I know so little about military life that my help won't be worth much, but I will do what I can." Then she wrapped her arms around his shoulders and squeezed.

Stumped by her reaction, Jason returned the hug, his arms tugging her close enough that he could smell her shampoo. She was close enough to kiss, but there was no romance in the room.

He'd killed that by making her cry with his sad story.

When she eased back, Angela's face was composed. "Post-traumatic stress. Is that what caused your retreat at Domino Park?"

Okay. This was another peeve. People who wanted to diagnose him without all the facts.

"Not really. I don't know. If it makes you feel better to call it that, go ahead." Jason held up his hands. "I don't have to put a label on every little thing. I lost a leg. I can't do everything you want. Now you know. Now you have to decide how to deal with it. This is why I don't talk about it." His pulse was pounding. The anger was there, but it wasn't wild or unfocused. Every word was razor-sharp. "The few people who know? They don't need a diagnosis."

"Because they've had the same experiences," Angela said. "They've been there. I'm glad you have someone who can listen the way you want."

That was a stinging blow. Was he being unfair? She'd reacted as he'd expected. This was the result he'd feared, and it hurt worse than he'd believed it could. Confusion. Anger. And loss. It was a bad mix.

"This weakness is new to me. When it catches me off guard like that and I fall, there's this instant anger that boils up. I need to put myself back together to get rid of it. Sometimes that means a quiet, cool place." Always. It always meant a place like a cave, but Angela didn't need to know that. He'd hit her with enough. "Let's end this topic for today." Once he'd absorbed this, he'd have more patience for all her questions.

"Having a body that lets you down might be new to you, but a lot of us mere mortals have to learn how to handle falling gracefully. I do it often enough I know the drill. Laugh no matter how much it hurts, brush yourself off and dance like it never happened. You should try it."

Stung, Jason started to argue and then snapped his mouth shut.

She didn't understand him.

"Says the woman who doesn't need any man." Jason snapped his fingers. "Oh, except for the 'adventure coach' who will be able to accomplish that most important thing of all. Not parasailing. Not bungee jumping or skydiving or swimming with sharks, because you will never do those things. How do I know? I know because you don't want to do them. If you did, you would already have shown the world. You moved away from your family to build the career you love. You don't need anyone's company for something you want badly enough."

Angela tilted her chin up. "What about the most important thing? What's that?"

"Proving it to your ex-husband." Jason leaned back, ready for her to disagree. "That's what you really want. The captain would have worked very well for that. A busted-up old vet who can't manage to dance and chew gum at the same time won't impress the ex."

It was the thing he'd been most afraid of all along. He'd spent entirely too much time thinking about a woman who could do better whenever she liked.

"Well." Angela stood and held out a hand when he made a move to follow her. "No need to walk me out."

"Guess that's a good thing," Jason snapped, ready to argue. The tension between them was wrong. "For someone who showed up without an invitation, you're in a big hurry to leave." The throbbing in his head matched his leg.

"You've made it clear you've got other plans now." Angela moved closer to the door. Was she ever going to meet his eyes? "I hope the things you love don't cause you any falls, Jason. Have fun at the birthday party." She shut the door quickly and he was left with silence.

Birthday party?

He rested his head against the cushion behind him, the familiar paint job the only distraction he could see.

Then he remembered Mira saying something about a niece or a nephew or both having a party at an arcade.

Angela assumed he was going with Mira because…

Jason pinched his nose in his best imitation of his mother.

Then it hit him with a flash. She thought he and Mira were dating.

If they were a couple, she had every reason to play off all the conversations they'd had because… What had she said?

"Everything has changed." He'd taken that as a comment on his leg. She'd meant his friendship with Mira.

Angela had read more into Mira's conversation than he'd realized.

And he didn't have her phone number to clear it up.

Since she'd never asked for his number, either, Jason had to decide whether he wanted to keep pushing this thing between them. Pushing usually led him to a hard fall.

CHAPTER SIXTEEN

BY THE TIME she made it home from Concord Court, Angela was exhausted. For a relatively short drive, she'd had plenty of time to swing through a wide range of emotions.

Okay. Two emotions.

Anger had arrived first. It had jumped into the passenger seat as she'd turned over the ignition, and it had never left. She didn't need a lecture about rearranging her life to prove something to her ex-husband. It was silly. Worse, if she'd done so, it could have been so much fun to have Jason along for the ride.

He'd been right. She didn't need him.

His own inability to see that his leg was no reason to sit out life… That was what turned up the heat under her temper.

He was afraid of his own feelings. She should have said that.

Not that it mattered. Not anymore.

And then disappointment chimed in from the back seat on the drive home. She'd anticipated more time with Jason, a guy who made benches exciting.

No matter how many times she tried to convince herself that Jason and Mira made sense together in a way the two of them didn't, disappointment elbowed back in.

"There's got to be a way to chase this mess away," she muttered to herself as she unlocked her door. A long Saturday night of wrestling with anger and disappointment would be terrible.

As she paced in front of the television, she turned her phone over and over, as if it was the talisman with the answer.

"In the movies, it's always girls' night out. That's the answer for man troubles." She grimaced at "man troubles" coming out of her own mouth.

How weird would it be to call her crush's mother to ask if she wanted to go out?

Since Mae Ward was the only face that came to mind when she pictured all the local contacts in her phone, she shrugged and found her number. "Can't be any stranger than driving to Concord Court without an invitation. You are really broadening your dating skills today." She made herself into a tiny ball, the world's smallest target, while the phone rang. If Jason and Mae were discussing her unexpected visit to a guy who had found a great girl or replaying their argument, she did not want to know.

"Why, Angela, I was just talking about you." Mae cleared her throat. It was easy to picture her pointing at the phone to show Jason who she was talking to. "What can I do for you?"

Two quick choices sprang to mind.

She could pretend this was an accidental pocket dial, end the phone call and go hide in the bathroom.

Or she could do what she'd called to do. "Mae, I know this is short notice, but I have two tickets for a mermaid show with dinner included. Would you be interested in going with me? They're for tonight." She had them because she'd purchased them while Jason was in the shower, just in case she needed to have actual plans to back up whatever lie she told him to get out of there with her pride intact. The sports car tour she'd originally planned to claim was way too rich for her cover story.

The long pause concerned her.

"I couldn't think of anyone else who would enjoy this like you would, Mae." That much was true. Jason's mother didn't let things like what other people thought bother her.

"Well, now, that's very sweet." Mae cleared her throat. "Do I need a swimsuit?"

Angela laughed. "No, we aren't part of the show. If you'll text me your address, I'll pick you up."

"I'd love to, but I've already made plans with this new fella I met on the singles' cruise." There was a pause. "I'm guessing Jason's a no-go on this one, is that right?"

Angela sighed. "We need a break from each other for a minute." She'd said it to keep his mother happy. Then she realized it was true. He had to get a handle on his own issues, and she would prove to the whole world and Jason Ward that she'd meant what she said all along. She could be happy on her own. "But that's okay. When you have some time, let's get out our calendars. I really do want to go parasailing. If you're up for being my partner, I want to do it." She would spike this particular ball for the whole world, both men who'd said she'd never do it, to see.

Mae gasped. "Oh, honey, you'll be so happy you did. Next week okay? I don't know what you have to do to get ready for school, but I am purely dying to get back up in the air."

Relieved, Angela smiled. "Let's do it Monday. I'll book it and send you the time. How's that?"

"Fabulous! Now you go out and have yourself a big time, sweet girl," Mae said. "You won't always be single, hon. Better do everything you dreamed of while you got the free time. That's my philosophy."

Angela was pleased as she ended the call. Before she could second-guess her intentions, she found the website and paid for the parasailing tour of the Bay. Some of the bad emotions were receding.

Then she realized she was heading out to watch a mermaid show on her own.

And she was fine with it.

What did a person wear to a mermaid dinner theater?

If Greer was here, she'd moan about how silly the whole thing was. It might be, but there was no way Nashville, even with as many charms as Music City claimed, had a mermaid dinner theater.

So she slipped on the dress she would have chosen for a date, if she were so inclined, and picked out her most comfortable sandals. Angela plugged the address into her phone and settled behind the wheel.

And her own gasp of happy surprise filled the car as she turned into the parking lot. Triton's Theater was over the top in the way that only the very best tourist traps can be. The billboard pointing the way to the door featured a beautiful mermaid with shimmering blue-green scales on her tail. Since there was not much of a building, the billboard was a necessary hint on how to get into the place. Angela immediately stepped into an elevator that took her down. Under the sea. The walls were glass with a view of the growing depths of water, but it had to be the best theme-park illusion.

Didn't it?

After she was seated, she glanced around. One corner of the room featured a sunken ship with eerie lights. Columns of coral were scattered here and there, and the walls were covered in murals featuring sea life. If it were possible to have fabric tablecloths in an underwater restaurant, it would look just like this place. "I have to take pictures."

She was still laughing as she placed her dinner order. Maybe it wasn't "authentic" water, but this was exactly her speed as far as sand and water went.

The lights dimmed and a loud splash clouded the water in the tank that took up the center of the room. When the three mermaids struck a pose, Angela picked up her phone and immediately took a picture. The show was a mix of synchronized swimming, campy theatrics, lights and music. About halfway through, Angela gave up counting how many mermaids were in the tank. They had to rotate in and out, but it all happened so seamlessly that it was impossible to tell where one actor ended and the next began. After a ten-minute performance, the music trailed away and the house lights came back up as Angela's waitress slipped her plate in front of her.

"That was amazing," Angela said. "Can

you even imagine the career path that leads you to becoming a performing mermaid?"

The waitress shrugged. "That's not something you train for. Life and luck brings you to the job."

"Yeah. And really, that's how the best jobs work, right?" Angela said as she examined her plate. "Seafood. Seems like a strange choice. What if the mermaids stage a swim-out in protest?"

"You here by yourself tonight, honey? Did you get stood up?" The waitress's smile was there, but Angela would have called it "playing along." She probably listened to similar jokes every day she showed up to work.

"No," Angela said as she picked up her water glass, "this is just for me."

"Don't see too many singles, mainly happy women and bored men, but you enjoy your meal. If you want a little more excitement above the water, we've got free tickets for a haunted boat tour. You can see some wrecks and ruins, one or two unexplained phenomena, and hear some great stories." The waitress held out a ticket. "My boyfriend's the captain. He does a much better ghost than King Triton. Want one?"

Angela nodded. She hated ghost stories. Like, even more than sand, but this was an opportunity.

By the time this show was over, a full twenty minutes of spectacle that involved a romance between two merpeople, lots of exciting lights and music, a mediocre tilapia entrée and a complimentary slice of key lime pie, Angela was more content with her life and choices than she had been in a while.

No daughter to whine about missing her favorite podcast or whatever.

No husband to explain the literary fallacies conflating sirens with mermaids.

Just the ability to grin and wonder at a wide, weird world she hadn't known existed before that night.

All that was left was to find an awesome caption.

"Does this seashell bring out my eyes?" she muttered as she made the short drive to Captain Dave's Spooky Swamp Tour. "Zumba until your fins fall off." The last tour of the evening, the one that all the big spooky fans wanted to be on was about to leave. She quickly typed, New water aerobics class. Think I'm going to like it. She put up a few of the pictures and then dropped her phone in her purse.

This time, there were no signs pointing the way. There was very little light until the boat appeared out of the darkness. This captain was dressed like he'd helmed an eighteenth-century whaling ship, even in the Florida heat.

He helped her down into the boat. Angela handed her ticket to a young girl dressed as if she'd been first class on the Titanic. "If you're going to take photos here, you might want to do it now. We're headed out into the darkness." Her monotone delivery. Was that intentional? Angela shook with an almost delighted shiver. She hated ghost stories. But apparently ghostly actors thrilled her.

"All three of us, one selfie." The girl held out her hand, so Angela fished out her phone and then moved to stand behind her. The captain loomed. That was the only description she could come up with. When she saw the photo, she understood. He was almost out of the frame.

As if no one knew he was there to include him in the shot.

Like a ghost. Woo-hoo.

"I'm going to post this with 'Made a new friend.' Is that good?"

The downside to being on her own was that she couldn't pretend she was doing anything other than talking to herself.

The old-timer in the seat next to hers tipped his head to the side. "Good, sure. But great?" He leaned forward. "Try 'Anybody seen my boo-y-friend?' Because he's a ghost, and you're by yourself. Get it?"

Yeah. She got it. He didn't have to point it out, though. Since this was her show, she went with her original idea and then squeezed into her seat. When she realized she was near the water, she almost tried to convince the old guy to switch. Dark plus the edge of the boat plus the unknown of the water plus the power of suggestion would equal a big case of the willies. Then she noticed the small panel of controls behind his shoulder.

Knowing the show was orchestrated would calm her nerves. Surely it would.

Before she could explain to the old-timer that good boo-y-friends were as difficult to find as real phenomena, the captain stood up and began his story. Now he had a thick

Massachusetts accent. Apparently, he'd been marooned, which meant left to die by his mutinous crew, on one of the unnamed keys in the year 1832. That was how he knew so much about the ghosts. He'd had a long time to meet them. The boat silently pulled away from the dock, each small ripple and shift in the water filling in the space between the growing darkness, and the cool breeze on the water sending a shiver down Angela's back.

"Already scared?" the old guy asked. "We haven't gotten to the good stuff yet."

Angela turned to say something, but saw him reach behind his shoulder. Foggy green light lit up the bottom of the boat and the Japanese couple in front of Angela gasped. She leaned closer to him. "Nothing to be scared of. I'm a fan of special effects." He shot a frown at her and held one finger over his lips.

For an hour or so, the captain talked. His stories were told in English first and then Spanish. The night was dark, but on the water, the moon shone brightly on deserted stretches of beach, the homes built above the water at Stiltsville, and along the old Florida homes grouped tightly together on the banks of the sheltered bay. More than once, she clamped down on nerves. The people on the boat didn't help. The gasps and shrieks that accompanied the light hitting a wispy shadow in the trees entirely too close to her side of the boat almost got to Angela, but she closed her lips tightly, certain the old guy was waiting for her reaction.

She might have nightmares for days. This was definitely a date activity. Someone alive and warm needed to wrap his arm over her shoulders and fast.

How they'd done this tour, with actors and special effects and whatever it was that could turn into a bouncing orb of light and the whispered word *beware* at the right time—it was good. Impossible to distill in pictures, but there was the idea for a poem that kept popping up. Something about finding the role you were born to play.

If she could figure out how to do it, she'd tell it in story form, maybe from the point of view of the star mermaid or the old guy working the controls. The images were so clear.

When the boat bumped up against the

dock and the lights came on, Angela met the old guy's stare.

"Knowing how it works didn't take all the shine off, did it? Go on, tell the truth." He tugged harder on his ball cap. "You can say something over and over. Don't mean you really believe it."

Angela tilted her head to the side. "You mean lie? Say the same lie over and over?" What else could it be if a person said something they didn't really believe?

"Didn't say you don't want to believe it." He tapped the panel. "You can say none of this is real. You see the panel. You don't want ghosts to be real." He grinned. "But nobody who believes that jumps the way you do at a flash of light and a good story."

As the captain helped her up on the dock, Angela realized there might be a poem there, too. About how some people can say all the right things but believe something they don't want to inside.

Eager to get to a pen and paper, Angela hurried back to her car. As she buckled her seat belt, her phone rang. She reached into her purse, so relieved whoever it was had waited until she was off the boat. The captain and his ghost helper might have tossed her overboard to join the spirits if she'd interrupted the show.

When she saw her daughter's name, she said, "Hey, baby, everything okay?"

"Are you out on a date?" her daughter shouted, her words garbled as if she was too excited to speak slowly. "There's only one way to get you on a haunted tour on a boat at night. You have company. A warm-blooded person to ward off the spirits. Remember that Halloween when you nearly brained the football team's quarterback because he showed up at the door dressed like Death? You hate that stuff."

Angela started the car. "I'm on a date with myself."

The stunned silence knocked her off balance. That was the story she'd decided on. She'd tell Greer she was enjoying her time and getting to know what she loved.

Greer wasn't buying it.

"You aren't on a date," her daughter said slowly. "You are out at night alone after dark on a boat, and no one knows where you are. Tell me how that's a thing we're doing now, Mom?"

Angela pulled out of the parking lot and considered that. Everything Greer said was fair. "I got a free ticket. It's not something I planned."

And now she might as well be sixteen and explaining why she'd missed curfew.

"I didn't enjoy it as much as I would have if you'd been with me." That was a line that might work if Greer used it on her, but Greer's snort communicated her opinion.

"You're just out to show you don't need anyone for anything, is that it?" Greer asked.

Angela was glad the roads were almost deserted. This was a conversation that would take concentration.

"No. It started out as one thing and changed in the middle. That's all. I went to the mermaid show because I wanted to. This was spontaneous. I was having fun, like you want me to, and I wanted to keep it going. I did that. I am safe. I am going home now." Angela hoped she was selling her side of the story.

"I told Dad you were on a date, so he should move you from the kids' table." Greer sighed. "I shouted it. Like a victory shout. I am so sorry. You're going to have to go through the whole 'don't need a plus-one' with him again."

Angela braked as she pulled into her garage and put the door down. She turned off the ignition and rested her head against the headrest. "Well, kid, you weren't entirely wrong. All I wanted on the ghost boat was some company, G. Going alone is not my thing. At all." But the problem was that she couldn't imagine herself on that dumb tour with anyone other than Jason. He would have made her laugh.

If she'd been with him, she'd have been too focused on him to worry about anything else.

Then she realized the old-timer had been right. All along, she'd been saying the right thing. Everything she'd said to Greer was right. She didn't need any man to be okay.

But she'd met the one man who made everything, even experiences she hated, better.

She'd also missed her window to do anything about it.

Jason was going to be better off after time with Mira.

"Are you home?" Greer asked quietly.

"I am." Angela opened her eyes. "And I realized, thanks to you and the old guy running the special effects, that I've been confused for too long."

Greer didn't answer.

"For a long time, I did things for you and for your father. When I took this job, I didn't have that. I've built a good career and told myself I was doing exactly what I wanted. And I was. I am happy, Greer."

Angela squeezed her eyes shut.

"But I met somebody along the way that changed some of that." Greer's gasp convinced her to speed up. "He's dating someone else, G. And it's fine. That's how this is supposed to work. You don't rearrange your life so that you can have anyone, so that you can be a couple and avoid the kids' table at weddings. Someone comes along who adds to what you want, instead of taking away."

Greer was quiet, never a good sign. Then she groaned, "He's dating someone else. Are you serious?"

Angela laughed. "Did you hear anything else I said because this is the good stuff. The good motherly advice."

"I already knew that, Mom. You've been

making me the hero of my own story forever. A date to the wedding? Him as the sidekick. That's all. Why do you have to make this so difficult?" Greer muttered, "It's because you haven't dated since you were expected to cut up a guy's steak for him or whatever."

"Again with the old," Angela said lightly, even if she didn't mean it.

"Okay." Greer cleared her throat. "There's no sense in worrying about the wedding anymore, except that I expect you to tell me about this guy when we're together again."

"And you'll drop this? The 'Mom needs a date' subject?" Angela asked. "We can go back to discussing who Greer should be dating."

Greer laughed. "Fine. And I'll tell Dad I was wrong. Fingers crossed you don't hear about it again."

Fingers crossed was nice, but Angela wouldn't count on it. Rodney would probably bring it up with the wedding toasts, how she almost messed up their seating arrangements and budget but her loveless state prevailed.

But she didn't say any of that out loud to Greer.

Maturity was a virtue.

"I'm going inside. I am home, safe and sound, but I will be sleeping with all the lights on. I hate ghost stories." Angela shivered as a cold breeze swept across her skin.

"What made you go?" Greer asked.

"All I could picture was how the posts would impress my friends." Angela shook her head. "I'm definitely going to need to get a handle on that impulse."

"Love you, Mom."

Angela was smiling as she walked into her kitchen. Her notebook was on the kitchen counter, ugly-cute spiders doodled in the margins of her latest work. She flipped the page and wrote down "A Modern Mermaid's Résumé" and hoped that would be enough to jog her memory.

Then she started a list of the things people said they believed, which might be different closer to the bone.

She'd been saying she didn't need a man in her life. That was true.

Closer to the bone, where the truth lived, Angela thought there might be something else.

She might not need any man, but imagining life without Jason even on the edges could bring on another shiver. Whatever that feeling was, only poetry could capture it.

CHAPTER SEVENTEEN

JASON GOT DRESSED on Monday and wondered what sort of day it would turn out to be. While he stood in front of the closet, pressing the button-down shirt he'd picked for the day, his phone rang.

"Mornin', Mama. How are you? Did you have a good brunch yesterday?" She'd been out with the same guy two days in a row. If they moved on to day three, he was going to have to determine whether he approved or not.

"You want to know a man? Take him out for mimosas. I swear, I never saw anything like it. The man loosened his bow tie at the table." His mother's scandalized delivery relieved some of Jason's concern.

"Not his bow tie. Anything but that." Jason couldn't guess at the proper brunch behavior, but he'd never wear a bow tie anywhere. No worries about loosening it in the wrong spot. His mother's hard line against neckwear at the brunch table made him wonder if he was the one out of step with dating. "Is that against brunch etiquette? What if he needed the ground rules explained? Not every man brunches."

"Well," his mother said, "we agreed we could see other people. He's not the worst I've met here, but surely he ain't the best, either. Handsome, sure. Good dresser, even if he's loose with the standards sometimes, but so dull. Just boring. Can't feature spending more than a meal with him, but nice enough."

He hadn't decided how to handle his mother dating.

Listening to her rundown of the attributes of every guy, especially the fails, was going to be difficult. Time to change the subject.

"Okay, what plans are you calling to convince me to join in today?" Jason smoothed a bit of lint off one sleeve and then turned off the iron.

"You wouldn't come with me anyway, but your favorite teacher and I are going parasailing. Together. Eat your heart out." His mother's crow would have made him smile, but he realized something important.

"Do you have Angela's phone number?" Ever since she'd left his townhouse, he'd been telling himself he could camp out in front of her office and then telling himself he'd do no such thing. Even if he wasn't dating Mira, that didn't mean he and Angela were a good fit.

That didn't change the fact that he owed her an apology.

"I do. When you stomped off at Domino Park, we exchanged numbers. I was hoping for a lunch date where I could sell her on all your strengths. She called me Saturday, and I couldn't go with her to this theater thing, but we made plans for today. I'm excited. If you wanted to 'run into her,' you know where she'll be about ten o'clock."

This time, her tone was sly.

"We aren't exactly on friendly terms right now." Jason eased down on his bed.

"Your fault?" his mother asked. "Because I warned you your skills need work."

Jason cleared his throat, certain he should not provide her any more details. "Would you give me her number if I asked?"

She sniffed. "I will not. Us ladies have to stick together. There's a whole lot of dangerous men in this world." Before he could take offense to that, she added, "But I will text your number to her. If you ask me nicely. You should have already moved on this, son."

Was he going to ask for his mother's help with getting a date?

"I'll think about it." Jason sighed. "First, I've got to go meet with Reyna, tell her why I'm not qualified for the job she wants me to take and how she'd be much better off hiring someone who feels less sorry for himself, and then I'm going to take the job. If she insists, I'm going to work here at Concord Court, helping vets looking for jobs, and I'm going to take an introductory social work class next semester." He hadn't discussed this with his mother, but he'd weighed everything he knew about himself and Sawgrass and veterans, and even late at night, he couldn't shake the idea that he was on the right path here. He'd go a few steps down it and regroup if he had to. Cautious optimism. That was where he'd settled in.

"Not accounting. Thank heavens," his

mother drawled. "I was sure it was wrong, so I told you to do it, knowing you'd march off in the other direction, but you haven't been yourself. I was afraid the current would sweep you along and you'd end up somewhere you hated, with one of them complicated adding machines and a sharp pencil."

She was quiet for a minute. "You can help veterans. With the right education, you could help a lot of people, son. You're onto something now."

The bubble of giddy relief at hearing her verdict surprised him and gratified him. It was impossible not to understand what a blessing she'd been his whole life, how lucky he'd been to have his parents and the career he'd had and even to have decades stretching in front of him to fill with whatever he pleased. It was a lot. Sunshine and bouncing notes and Motown and Smokey all flowing through him.

"I better get to it." Jason forced himself to slow down. The burst of adrenaline that hit when he knew he was doing the right thing had made his hand shake.

"Yes, you better." His mother's smile beamed through the phone.

Jason hung up, but before he could slip the phone into his pocket, it dinged to alert him to a text.

While you're on a roll, think on this, too.

His mother's text was followed by a photo of him and Angela dancing in Domino Park. Before the disaster. His mother had caught the second he'd pulled Angela closer so he could talk to her. Her head was bent toward his, long brown hair draped over her shoulders and back, but it was easiest to see his face. He'd been caught up by her. Focused. It was no wonder he'd stumbled. He hadn't been able to look away from her.

Without thinking too much, which was what got him into trouble in the first place, Jason moved to the social media site Angela had shown him, the one he'd checked now and then to see whatever she posted. He made his own account and posted the photo, adding a poem underneath. The poem being the one surefire way to catch her attention. He texted his mother a link to the post. Make sure she sees this.

Then he shoved his phone in his pocket.

He had a meeting, an actual meeting with a time and a place, so he took two extra minutes getting ready and decided to cut through the pool area to Concord Court's office.

Reyna Montero wanted to meet with him. The time had come to give her a final answer. His other plan had been to see if Angela was in her office. Now he had a real deadline. He had to be at Domino Park by one o'clock. This shouldn't take long.

He'd say, "Don't hire me."

Reyna would say, "I'm going to hire you."

And that would be settled.

Then he opened the door and found a group waiting for him. Reyna was there. She discreetly checked her watch when he walked in, so he was glad he'd planned to be five minutes early. Her face would not show approval, but if he'd been late, she would have made sure he understood. Career military. They understood each other already.

The only other person in the room he recognized was his therapist. Michelle was seated across from Reyna's desk and she gave him a head nod in hello.

"Let's get started." Reyna pointed him to

the only available seat and plopped down behind the desk. "This is Eric Westinghouse,
the head of the social work department at
Sawgrass. I get the impression you were already supposed to have introduced yourself,
but Westinghouse has no idea who you are."
She paused and stared from Jason to Westinghouse, and Jason got the message. He
offered his hand to shake. When that was
taken care of, Reyna continued, "And this
is my sister, Brisa. She's going to be helping
out here at Concord Court, so I've invited
her to sit in."

"Assistant manager, not that Reyna wants
to give me the title." The younger woman
seated catty-corner to Reyna stretched
over to shake his hand. The faint scent of
something sweet, suntan lotion or expensive shampoo, accompanied her movement.
No doubt about it, Brisa Montero knocked
grown men out with one smile on a regular
basis. Eric Westinghouse sighed when she
returned to her seat.

Brisa was beautiful, but he couldn't imagine her signing up for a haunted boat tour
or lecturing about the joy of the perfect
first line of poetry. Angela was mesmeriz-

ing. The passion she had for teaching and learning new things, those were real, part of who she was and always would be.

He was hooked.

Unable to look away.

"I called everyone here today because we need an organized plan for career counseling. Michelle and I have been discussing this, and we agreed we've got the right candidate here." Reyna turned to Jason. "That's you. What do you say? You promised me you'd help if you could." Then she tilted her head down to await his response.

The urge to fidget under her stare was strong. So strong. But he couldn't help asking for more information. "I don't have any counseling experience or a degree." He motioned at Eric Westinghouse. "I don't even know what is involved because I haven't done my homework yet."

He didn't glance at Michelle. There had to be some kind of confidentiality clause that would keep her from exposing him. Didn't there? Or did everyone already know he and Michelle had discussed how this could work?

"If there are people who come through

needing in-depth help, we'll set them up with counseling sessions." Michelle waved a hand. "What we need is someone with critical-thinking skills, good listening and writing skills, and the ability to operate a computer to assist people with searches. Reyna wants to open this up to all vets, not just Concord Court. Everything's online these days. Most everyone that comes through will know the basics, but we can give them a head start."

Eric Westinghouse leaned forward. "We can start with aptitude tests to help people who are struggling to find their way. I have a lot of information on government-sponsored and not-for-profit programs that can help with a variety of challenges. Classes for hard skills in new software. Funding for nontraditional programs. Grants to support small business. Anyone can make those referrals if they have the information they need at hand. What we require is a contact, someone who can be trusted by the men and women who land at Concord Court. I expect someone who has walked in their shoes could be a welcome sight."

When everyone's gaze swung in his direction, Jason couldn't even pretend he hadn't spent hours weighing the job. "I want to, but only if I'm the right guy for this." He wiped both hands on his jeans. Sweaty palms surprised him. This was a low-risk situation. Saying no would be easy enough. He had no obligation to say yes.

Except he could help people who needed it.

He could do something that mattered without upsetting his mother or getting a degree in accounting.

And he could get a taste of what this career might be from the inside. If he hated it, he could save himself time and money.

But if he enjoyed it and was good at it, he could go on and get the degrees he needed while he worked.

He shrugged. "I guess I could give it a try." When Reyna's frown turned into a scowl, he cleared his throat. "Sorry. I tend to downplay things when I'm nervous, but I'd very much like to have this job. I've been floating along because none of the usual paths fit me. It's frustrating. For years, I've had work to do, a clear job, but now... I can understand how people get into trouble. I want to help. This is where I'd like to take my shot." He shifted in his seat. "I've had a few ideas I could run by Michelle or Eric. Small groups for Concord students going to Sawgrass or set up monthly for anyone who wants to drop in, whether they have a job or need a different one. Just a place to talk about the transition from military work to civilian."

Reyna nodded while Brisa sparkled at him. It was hard to call what she did a smile, because it gleamed.

"Do you have time to follow me back to my office?" Eric asked. "I brought all kinds of information on the programs you'll need for job counseling, but I didn't bring a thing regarding social work." He clapped a hand on Jason's shoulder. "Believe me, a guy with your background could do so much good in this case."

Jason tapped his foot on the floor and wondered if it could be that simple. "I have a job." He tasted, no savored the words.

"And I'll help you pick some classes for the fall semester. Registration opens on Friday." Eric leaned back. "Unless you have them chosen already."

"Keep me out of the language building," Jason muttered. Whatever happened between him and Angela, he didn't want to put it on hold for an entire semester because he was reading British literature.

"Well, Spanish would be a big help, but okay. You don't have to learn a new language." Eric rubbed his hands together. "Introduction to Social Work is happening this fall. That could be a good place to start. I'm not teaching it, but it gives a good foundation for all the things you can do with the degree."

Jason offered him a hand to shake again. "I had that one on my list. I'll do it, professor. Thanks so much for the suggestion. If it's all right, I'll drop by on Friday when I'm at registration."

Eric shook hands and then stood. "Do you need my office number?" He rummaged in his pockets. "Why do I never have a business card when I need one?"

Jason waved a hand and very obviously did not look at his therapist. "I'm sure I can find it."

Eric pointed at a box near the desk. "We can talk over what I brought, too. There's a paper with websites listed, and several books you can loan out to people who need direction on where to start job hunts, résumés, that kind of thing. If you have a minute, take a look at them." He gave a quick wave and then stepped outside into the heat.

Brisa stood. "Want to see your office?"

His office? Jason glanced quickly around the room, as if someone was going to jump out and yell "surprise."

"It's the shared space I showed you. For all of our programs, I have that office set aside so that my contractors can meet with their clients in a neutral space." Reyna pointed down a short hallway opposite the door. "It's a desk. There are filing cabinets. I'll give you your own locked drawers, but it's not *your* office."

"*Our* office, I suppose I should say," Brisa said over her shoulder as she led him down the hallway. "Until Reyna agrees I'm here to work instead of to desert her when she needs me most, I won't get my own real estate, either. So far, only Sean and Reyna rate their own dedicated spaces, but we can dream, right?"

She flashed the megawatt smile at him

again and then strode out confidently like a model.

Jason stopped inside the door, hands on his hips as he surveyed the space. It was clean. Minimal. The desk was modern to match the decor, and a computer was set up right in the middle.

"It doesn't have a lot of personality, but it will get the job done." Michelle was propped against the doorjamb behind him. "Congrats on the job."

"I can't believe it's that easy. I should buy a lottery ticket today," Jason said.

"Everything is coming up Jason." Michelle stepped inside. "It would be a good day to go after the brass ring, the final frontier, the moon."

Jason absorbed that as he moved to sit behind the desk.

Michelle arranged an imaginary hat on her head. "Therapist hat. How does the fact that Reyna, a decorated veteran with nothing but the highest honors, respects you enough to ask you to come work here..." She studied his face. "How does that make you feel? She knows your whole story, right? The accident. The amputation. The difficulty you've been having getting your life started. Is there a piece she's missed?"

"You know I understand that this is a problem I created in my head, this expectation that other people would pity me or worse. I've let it mess up my life enough already." He drummed his fingers on the desk and realized everything he was saying was correct. It had all been in his head. All of his problems loomed large enough to keep him stuck in one place in fear, but they were mostly imaginary what-ifs that were never going to come true. "The next time I visit my therapist, I need to talk to her about the ways I shoot myself in the foot, do dumb stuff to protect my delicate feelings from something that might never come."

Michelle pretended to make a mental note. "You aren't all that unusual, you know. So many people do that, tell themselves they can't want something, whatever it is that you're thinking about now, because they're afraid of how badly it will hurt if they're disappointed." She cleared her throat. "So many people. Good people. All the people in this room, in fact." She grinned when he glanced up. "Yeah, if you decide to go into social work or therapy, do not do it because you believe you'll have all the answers for your own life. My therapist had to teach me that." She took off her imaginary hat and tossed it on an imaginary hat rack. "The best news I have for you is, whatever you've messed up, you have time to fix it."

Jason stared hard at his hands. He could. All it would take was swallowing his pride, and at this point, he should have enough experience that he could make it go down easy.

"I have a new job. I have a plan for the fall semester. My townhouse is comfortable. All of that I owe to Reyna and Concord Court." Jason tried to remember the last time he was so calm, so certain that everything was going to work out for him.

Michelle held up her hand to tick off points. "The leg is healing. You're making friends in a new town. You are running again, something that was important to you. It's almost as if all those things we talked about in our first session, the ones you were afraid were never going to come and you'd be left a miserable lump on the sidelines, have fallen into place. Did a wise person tell you they would?" Before he could answer, she waved both hands. "Never mind. As your therapist, I would never say it as plainly as that." She tapped a finger to her chin. "There's still something missing, though. What could it be?"

Jason cleared his throat. "A therapist who says 'I told you so.' I'm amazed." He stood. "The relationship. You said it should come last."

She blinked slowly. "I did? That doesn't sound like me."

Jason chuckled. "Okay, maybe I said that. And she showed up out of order." He scrubbed both hands over his face. "I wasn't ready."

Michelle grinned. "Yeah, okay. Get ready." Then she turned on her heel and walked out. "See you later this week. I expect progress."

Should he be mad? Maybe. She had to be breaking some kind of rule regarding his client privilege.

It was hard to be mad when he understood more with every tick of the clock that she was right. There was still time. Not quite eleven o'clock. Plenty of time to make it to

Domino Park to find out whether Angela would even listen to what he wanted to say.

Brisa stuck her head into the room. "Everything okay in here?"

"Perfect. Just perfect." Jason trotted toward the lobby's front door, and the pinch of the prosthesis, which had definitely never been built for movements like that, stopped him. He braced himself against the wall and twisted his leg, impatient with the pain. "Come on, leg. Don't make me replace you with my robot hardware."

Brisa raised both eyebrows. "Interesting."

He didn't have time to explain, so the story tumbled out. "Injury from my time in the service. I have the wrong prosthesis on for running, but I want to go fast."

She stepped back and hugged the wall to make plenty of room. "Then let me get out of your way. *Walk* fast. That's just about as good in my experience." She pointed at the sandals she was wearing, the heels sky high. "No running in these, either."

Jason pointed at the office as he limped around her. "I'll be back tomorrow. I want to go through the files that Westinghouse left and set up a schedule."

Brisa pursed her lips. "Good plan. Jot this down on your list. Find out how much you'll be paid." Then she raised her eyebrows, the twinkle in her eyes almost as dangerous as the sparkle that came with every smile. She was a knockout, but she was wasting his time right now.

"Good note. Thanks!" Jason walked as fast as he could toward the door and wished he'd driven his truck that morning. Maybe he should switch prostheses. The urge to run would not go away.

"It's what I do. Fill in the details," Brisa called out as he stepped through the door. The heat hit him in the face and sweat beaded up immediately but he didn't slow down his determined, although slower than he wanted, walk.

Soon he'd ask about an upgraded everyday alternative to this prosthesis. This was his life. He had to be able to live it.

After hours and hours that were probably minutes, he slid behind the wheel of his truck. This time he knew where he was going. He knew what he was going to do. Through all of it, this was the piece he'd been missing. The leg, the job, the classes—

all of it was secondary to this. He pulled out of the parking spot, ready to find the woman who would make it all matter.

CHAPTER EIGHTEEN

ANGELA NERVOUSLY TAPPED out a pattern on the paper bag she held in her lap and tried to soak in the peace of the bench under the banyan tree. It was a beautiful day. She had shade. Over her shoulder, people played dominoes. Occasionally, snippets of conversation floated in her direction, but it was only background noise.

When Mae showed her Jason's post, Angela hadn't had a good response, but she didn't want to discuss all of the back-and-forth with Jason. He'd said some things that pinched, but most of all, he'd moved on. What was this about?

"But you're still sitting here, aren't you?" Angela muttered and tried again to squash the hope that this meant another chance. It kept popping up.

"If you want people to avoid this bench, talking to yourself is a good plan." Jason slid down on the bench next to her and straightened his left leg out with a wince. She'd seen him do the same thing enough times to be annoyed with herself that she'd never asked about it. Not once.

"I don't know if these sandwiches are as good as the ones we had before," Jason said as he put a bag between them, "but I promised lunch."

Angela waved the bag she'd clenched with both hands. "I brought dessert." She pulled out her phone. "Let's talk about that promise." She pulled up his post to read, "'Roses are red, and they're pretty in a bunch, meet me in the park at one, and let's do lunch.'" She frowned. "You already have more likes than I ever get and you started the account today. How?"

He shrugged. "Poetry. That has to be the answer." He held up one finger. "Rhyming poetry. Have you ever tried it? People really enjoy the rhyme."

Angela rolled her eyes, her reluctant chuckle a relief. She'd been so worried they'd never get back to this easy type of conversation after their argument. "Does Mira know about all this?"

"Nope, but I'll tell her. I'll tell all the guys around the pool." Jason stretched an arm along the bench, his hand resting against her back. The pose was familiar but different. "I'm going to talk to my friends about all the great things that happened to me today. Mira is a friend. A good friend. She kicks me out of my rut, but that's all. I didn't realize you thought we were dating until after you left." The smooth tug on her hair as he rubbed strands between his finger and thumb was...

She shook her head. He was stealing her breath right there. "How did it all go so wrong, that last conversation?" This was important. She needed the answer, but his touch drew her closer.

This time she didn't have to worry about keeping space between them.

"When you said everything changed, I assumed you meant my leg. I couldn't do all the things you wanted to do to show your ex you were better off without him." As she studied his face, she could see nothing but open emotion. He wasn't hiding anything. "I was lashing out because sometimes I do that, but I'm doing all the right things to get over that. My therapist told me so."

His virtuous pose made her smile, which was what he wanted. He brushed a strand of hair off her cheek before she knew it was bothering her. Almost as if it was one of those subconscious habits that you might pick up over a lifetime of love with someone.

Was this going to be a thing? The urge to stand up and pace was strong as she made her case, but she didn't want to break their connection.

She wanted to be in that kind of love, the one where she was so comfortable with another person that she showed it without thinking.

Angela closed her eyes. Love. No one had said anything about love between them yet. They'd just started speaking again.

Well, he was speaking. She wasn't doing much to hold up her end of the conversation.

"You have a therapist. I have an old guy on a ghost tour." Angela nodded as he raised an eyebrow. "I was saying what I thought was right. I don't need a date to the wedding, a man around, to be happy. I don't. I can do whatever I put my mind to, with or without you, Jason Ward." She watched his frown form. "But now that I found you, I want you around. You make everything better."

"Even with the falls and the moods and the…" His eyebrows shot up. "I do have a job now. I'll be a job counselor at Concord Court. I'm also going to explore social work as a degree, so I'm not without some plans."

Angela tilted her head to the side and realized he was waiting for her verdict. He was nervous he wasn't good enough for her?

"Jason. Listen." She licked her lips as she considered her words and every thought evaporated as his stare locked on her mouth. That kiss. They were going to have it. Finally. "I believe you can do anything you want to. I have always believed that. The day we met at the administration building? I was pretty sure you could beat those kids at their game and then melt their Frisbees down with the power of your mind. You give off this… It's a feeling I have. When you are around, I don't have to worry. Whatever comes at you, you can handle it." She shrugged a shoulder. "I don't know how to say it any other way. I can make plans. You can make whatever blows up those plans work. You could be a poet or an accountant or a soldier or whatever you decide. I've always known that."

"Can I be your plus-one to this wedding?" Jason asked, his lips curled up in a small smile. "I do not have a captain's uniform, but I'll buy a new suit."

Angela rested her head on his shoulder. "Rodney is going to flip when I change my answer."

"Then at least I'll have fulfilled part of my role." Jason's laugh rumbled under her ear.

"I couldn't re-create the whole day. No stage or loud salsa music, and no dancer yelling out steps," Jason said. "But I'm glad you came."

She tapped the bag of guava pastries she'd picked up. "I tried them already. They're not quite as good as the ones we had last time, but they're nice."

"You already ate one of these? The pastries you brought me as a gift?" Jason asked and then laughed out loud. "That might be worse than loosening your tie after too many mimosas."

"Is that rude? I didn't think you'd mind." She squeezed her eyes shut. It was rude. She'd sampled his pastries before giving them to him. Covering her eyes with her hands wouldn't make her invisible, but it might keep her from melting through the bench. "Your mother told me about Harry's tie, too. I didn't understand the problem. Maybe I'm not good at dating."

Jason moved the pastry bag aside and ran his hand under the fall of her hair to gently squeeze the tight muscles on her neck. Maybe she wouldn't die of embarrassment. She didn't want to miss his kiss. She could die after. "I was nervous, I guess. I'm sorry. Dating me will mean more missteps. There could also be skydiving. Mermaid theater. An opinionated teenage girl. The ex-husband who still takes up too much space in my head, his new wife and baby."

He repeated the slow massage across the aching muscles in her shoulders.

Angela crossed her leg and celebrated inside when he turned to watch the way her foot moved. They were going to be okay.

"With me, there will be literal missteps. Falling. Bruised egos and the occasional moody silence." Jason shook his head. "But I love family drama."

"No one loves family drama." Not that

she was overly worried about that. Whatever happened, everyone involved would be fine all the way through. That was how they'd managed to stick together so far. She had no plans of changing that. "But at this wedding, you'll be forced to tell your story early and often." She wanted to let him off the hook, even if the whole event would be so much better if Jason was there. It would be so nice to have someone there protecting her back.

"Listen, this is not something I ever expected to say, especially at this point, but I'm in. I want it all. Annoying ex, opinionated children. It's part of who you are."

Angela wrinkled her nose as she considered that. When he put it that way, her package deal was a lot less impressive.

But he was right.

"I mean, you've met my mother," Jason said and shook his head. "I can't sweep her under the rug."

"Are you going to tell me why you were limping when you got here or…" Angela didn't want to give another option. "It has to be okay for me to ask these things, Jason."

"Yeah." He exhaled slowly. "Honestly? I tried to run on the wrong prosthesis. I deserved the pinch. I have to learn how to work in this new body. Some days, when I've forgotten how things have changed and I'm my old self, taking jobs and in a hurry to get on with life, it's hard."

"It'll get easier." Angela believed it. All these things, his job and her family and the way he lived with his new body—it would all get better.

"I agree." Jason raised a hand to rest it under her chin, his thumb urging her head closer. Then he pressed his lips against hers, a sweet, sure, heated kiss with the heartbeat of a lifetime rolling underneath. He brushed his lips over hers and then teased her lips with his tongue. Angela squeezed his waist and relaxed into him as his arms tightened, raising a shiver of anticipation and soothing it at the same time.

"Roses are red, violets are blue, all I need is this bench and you." She wrinkled her nose up at him. "All my life I've been beating myself up to write poetry. Who knew it could be that easy?"

He shook his head. "Will I regret embracing that format? Only time will tell."

"It made me laugh," Angela said. "I love it. And it will always make me think of you."

"You love it." He tilted his head to the side. "Jury's still out on me?"

"Love at first sight. Writers and poets have embraced the concept, but I've never believed it." Angela smiled. "That day we met at Sawgrass? Your frown was not conducive to love at first sight. But a man who finds poetry in good music? I was helpless. All the rest of this has been me fooling myself. Love is like skydiving. Take the first step and then all you have to do is fall."

EPILOGUE

A few weeks later
Key West destination wedding

"I LIKE THE stand-and-sway music this DJ has chosen," Angela said as she danced next to Jason on the crowded dance floor.

"Can't get too wild. A yacht's dance floor is roughly the size of a walk-in closet," Jason murmured and thanked his lucky stars. If he fell here, the guy next to him would shove him upright. If he pushed too hard, the guy on the other side could correct.

"At least there's plenty of warm champagne to cool off with." Angela grinned up at him and blinked innocently. "I'm having the time of my life with you. Thank you for coming."

"So glad I didn't miss a thing, but you, in that dress… That's worth a whole lot of family drama."

"Which you enjoy." Angela raised an eyebrow. "You told me that. I've lost count how many times you've had to explain what happened to your leg."

"Running along the beach while you and Greer were snorkeling this morning increased my numbers." Jason rested his hands on her hips. "It gets easier."

"I'm glad." Angela brushed a hand over his shoulder. Every time she did that, touched him as if she'd done it a million times, the feeling settled deeper into his bones. He wanted that touch. He loved being able to meet her stare across a dinner table while her ex boasted how much the wedding was costing him, what with all the people they'd invited, and know that they were going to laugh about it later.

Or wandering along behind Angela and Greer while they cooed and coaxed one of Hemingway's cats closer. He hadn't understood half of what they said, but that shared language made them both so happy and drew him into their circle, so he couldn't complain.

"Want to make some trouble?" he asked and ran his hands over the bare skin of Angela's back. Her dress had surprised him, but she had come to make good on her original plan of showing everyone she was living her best life. The sexy dress was a solid point.

"With you? Always." She stretched up to press her lips to his.

* * * * *

For more great romances from acclaimed author Cheryl Harper, visit www.Harlequin.com today!

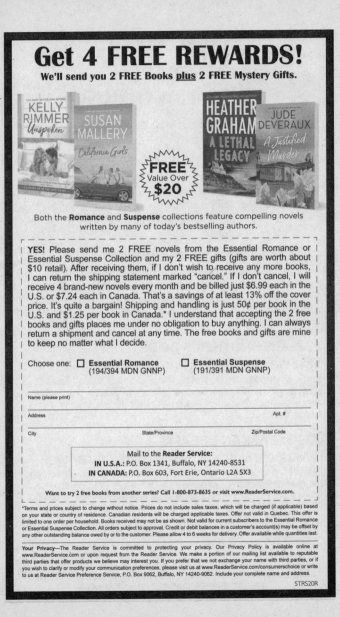